“I’d much rat[illegible] you than seek a potential wife. A woman I fully intend to marry only on paper. Show my father the male heir. Deed done.”

“Sebastian, how can you say that? Much as I care about you, it offends me that you’d treat a woman like that. And use a child in such a manner.”

“I don’t know how else to do this, Zee. Unless the perfect woman falls into my arms, I will be forced to find a facsimile wife to win the company. And I must win because L’Homme Mercier must remain as it is.”

He couldn’t know how hearing that devastated her. She could understand his desire to keep the family business as he wished it to remain. That his father had set such a ridiculous requirement was cruel to both his sons.

And that made her even more reluctant to reveal her news to him. He didn’t need to know. Well, he did. But he didn’t need to be a part of her life. Nor she his. That was optional. A choice she mustn’t allow to be wrong.

How could she possibly tell him she was pregnant?

Dear Reader,

This story started with a long-haired Highland cow. This is probably my idea of the perfect life, living somewhere between country and city. Falling in love with a man who will move worlds to make you happy. Jumping into all that life offers you. And add in a few chickens to keep that cow company.

It's no secret I love setting my stories in Paris. I've had the opportunity to visit a few times. The city dazzles me. And the French language captivates me (even if I can't understand a single syllable). So I hope you enjoy this adventure filled with surprises and enchanting moments.

Michele

Consequence of Their Parisian Night

Michele Renae

Recycling programs for this product may not exist in your area.

ISBN-13: 978-1-335-59660-4

Consequence of Their Parisian Night

This is a work of fiction. Names, characters, places and incidents are either the product of the author's imagination or are used fictitiously. Any resemblance to actual persons, living or dead, businesses, companies, events or locales is entirely coincidental.

For questions and comments about the quality of this book, please contact us at CustomerService@Harlequin.com.

Harlequin Enterprises ULC
22 Adelaide St. West, 41st Floor
Toronto, Ontario M5H 4E3, Canada
www.Harlequin.com

Printed in U.S.A.

Michele Renae is the pseudonym for award-winning author Michele Hauf. She has published over ninety novels in historical, paranormal and contemporary romance and fantasy, as well as written action/adventure as Alex Archer. Instead of "writing what she knows," she prefers to write "what she would love to know and do" (and yes, that includes being a jewel thief and/or a brain surgeon).

You can email Michele at toastfaery@gmail.com.
Instagram: @MicheleHauf
Pinterest: @toastfaery

Books by Michele Renae

Harlequin Romance

Cinderella's Second Chance in Paris
The CEO and the Single Dad
Parisian Escape with the Billionaire

Visit the Author Profile page
at Harlequin.com.

Praise for
Michele Renae

"Renae's debut Harlequin [Romance] novel is a later-in-life romance that's sure to tug at readers' heartstrings."

—*Library Journal* on *Cinderella's Second Chance in Paris*

CHAPTER ONE

"ABSOLUTELY NOT!"

The woman who'd flatly refused Sebastian's proposal and shoved the engagement ring he had just shown her back in his face, grabbed the car door handle and opened it. She thrust out a designer-shoe-clad foot toward the curb and then turned to look over her shoulder to waggle a finger in his face.

"You, Sebastian Mercier, are a rogue. You don't want to marry me because you love me. You just want to control your family's company. And I will not be bought. Oof! Men!"

With that, she fled the limousine in a rage of silk and silvery sequins, a burst of fluffy white marabou fluttering in her wake.

Sebastian leaned back and closed his eyes. That had been his second failed proposal in a six-month period. And he'd thought finding a wife would be easy!

Apparently, a man with money, a luxe Paris

home and social connections to everyone who was anyone wasn't motivation enough to entice a *yes* from a woman.

Well, he wasn't an imbecile. Women required an emotional commitment. A sparkly ring was not sufficient incentive.

He'd had to give it a go. He and Amie had dated for three weeks. Had seen each other every day. Had enjoyed great sex. As a fashion influencer followed by tens of millions, Amie had been a perfect candidate to step into the role of his wife. His family approved of her old money and fashion connections.

But…after a recent media leak, the competition between him and his brother, Philippe, was no longer secret. And such information tended to matter to some, especially if it affected their future. And their heart.

The refusal did not upset him as much as expected. He hadn't been in love. Nor, he suspected, had Amie. Theirs had been an affair of passion. Love must not intrude on such a cold business transaction. Love and the emotional attachment that came along with it must not interfere in his quest to find a bride.

Will you marry me and have my child so I can then take control of the family company?

Besides, what did love even feel like?

He'd try again when the opportunity presented

itself. He must. Philippe must not win. He'd regroup and begin the wife search again after—well, after a good, stiff drink. A man did have a right to mourn his loss, didn't he?

Tucking the ring box away in his suit coat pocket, he leaned across the seat to grab the open door when a woman's shout—in English—called for him to hold the door.

A stunning vision sprinted toward the limo. A floaty pale pink dress dazzled with glints and sparkles. And wearing that lovely creation was a beautiful blonde with arms spread in a plea to wait as she neared.

Sebastian leaned back just as the blonde plunged inside the car, changing the very air with her arrival. He felt suddenly lifted, and curious. She shoved a heap of purse—and some sort of clothing—onto his lap, blew out a panting breath, grabbed the door and closed it.

"Drive!" she demanded of his driver with the pound of a dainty fist against the seat. "Please! He's chasing me!" She swiped a dash of wavy hair from her eyes and her panicked look took him in. "I'm so sorry, but could you…just drive me a few blocks from here? There's a man. He's after me."

Gorgeous, pale blue eyes surrounded by the lushest black lashes frantically met his. "Someone is after you? Whom do I have to fight for your honor, my lady?"

"It's the photographer. He took off after me because I kicked him in the—"

Still panting from what must have been a high-speed run, she patted her chest. His protective instincts in high gear, Sebastian glanced out the back window. No sign of the perpetrator. He nodded to the driver to pull away. Why not play along with this interesting insertion of feminine audacity into the evening?

Her huffing breaths settled a bit as she nodded and patted his hand. "Thank you. I'll get out soon. I just need to put some distance between us."

"If you are in trouble…"

"You'd fight for my honor?"

"But of course, mademoiselle. My limo is at your disposal."

"I'll take a rain check on that fight. But don't think I won't forget the offer."

"Anything for a damsel in distress."

Her worried moue crinkled into a smile. Freckles that dotted her entire face got lost in a few of those crinkles. Cute.

"This is your limo? Oh, dash it. I'm really sorry about all this."

"Don't apologize. I've never had the opportunity to rescue a damsel before. This one will look good on my résumé, eh?"

She laughed and shook her head. "Oh, it will."

"If I may ask, why the kicking of something or other and the resultant dash?"

"Well." She smoothed out the sparkly skirt. "My girlfriend gave me a princess photo shoot as a treat," she said. "Because of the breakup, you know. I dated Lloyd for six months. I thought for sure he was going to propose. So that night at the fancy restaurant I asked if he wanted to have kids and he laughed. Hated kids! Can you believe it?"

Sebastian wasn't sure if she was angling for an answer or some kind of affirming gesture. But he didn't have time to shrug as she continued her breathless ramble. It seemed her fear was streaming out in words, and he wasn't about to stop her, especially since she was already fearful of one man.

"And then!" she continued dramatically. "Lloyd confessed he'd slept with my flatmate, who was also my boss at the flower shop. Who—let me tell you—had the audacity to insist I move out of our flat while *they* were away on vacation." She paused, winced. "Sorry. Too much information? Probably. I'm frazzled. Anyway! I was so excited about the photo shoot. It was a means to forget about that awful breakup. And this dress is so posh…" She spoke as quickly as he suspected she must have been running. "And look at my makeup and hair. I look like a princess, right?"

He nodded, unable to resist a smile. A princess with freckles and looking more like an imp lost in a glamorous world that was perhaps not her natural habitat. But what did he know? If she truly had been in danger, he was just thankful she'd jumped into the back of his car.

Azalea was rambling! It was a bad habit that always swooped upon her when she was nervous. Or afraid, as the case was. Though her fears were reduced knowing they were driving away from the scene of the crime. And the man sitting next to her seemed quite gentlemanly. So handsome. His dark hair was short but looked as though it deserved a good finger tousle. A sharp jawline and the hint of stubble suggested an elegance that matched the fitted black suit. Was that a glint of diamond on his cuff links? His look said corporate raider with a softer touch of international jewel thief. She loved a good heist movie with a charming rogue robber. And his eyes held genuine concern. Offering to rescue the damsel?

Yes, please!

"I can't imagine a life without kids and family, you know? I love children!" Azalea added, because she didn't want the man to think she was totally off her rocker.

Just stop rambling, then!

She nodded to her inner thoughts. Yes, shut up. And perhaps they'd driven far enough by now?

"Children are lovely," he offered with a bemused tone. "You seem to have calmed a bit. I hope the photographer did not do anything untoward?"

"Well." She sighed heavily. "He made terrible, lewd remarks. And he touched me! Not where a girl wants to be touched by a stranger, either. So I panicked."

It had all gone knees up when that sleazy photographer had slipped his mitts up under her skirt, insisting he was making an adjustment—and then he had gone too far.

Azalea had reacted. Her father had taught both her and her sister, Dahlia, if they ever felt unsafe around a man to kick first, ask questions later. And forget questions, actually. Just run. Which she had done.

"My dad taught me self-defense. My kicking skills are excellent. Got him right where it counts. Then I grabbed my stuff. And…"

She leaned back and blew out a breath. She'd made it away safely. Thanks to some quick thinking and maintaining her wits. Yet now the adrenaline rushing through her system made her jittery and she just wanted to go somewhere and cry.

No. She was stronger than that. Find a hotel to stay the night, and text Maddie about never recommending that photographer again, and then head back to Ambleside in the morning. The day had been a bust. No princess day for Azalea Grace, after all.

On the other hand, she had run into a rescuing knight.

"Tell me where they are and I'll take care of them both," Sebastian offered.

She shook her head. "I wish you had been around a few weeks ago when Lloyd broke it off. Oh, and now. I just...want to forget about this day." She grabbed her stuff from his lap. "Sorry. I've been rude. I'll pay you for the ride."

"No apologies necessary. What matters is that you are all right."

"I'm good."

"Can I drop you somewhere?" he asked.

"I...uh...was going to rent a hotel room for the night. My girlfriend and I spent the afternoon together. It was so good to see Maddie again. We grew up together. She headed to Paris the moment we finished our A levels. Anyway, she gave me a coupon for a hotel in the tenth arrondissement, I believe. It's in my purse somewhere." She began to dig inside her bag. "What an awful way to end what should have been a perfect day. I'm just…ooh, I need a drink, actually."

"I was just thinking much the same before you graced me with your presence. I have a proposal for you," he said.

"Yeah? Does it involve alcohol?"

"It could. It may also involve decadent treats and tiny hors d'oeuvres."

The way he said that, with a hint of a tease, made her smile. And nothing about him screamed lecher. The expensive suit—and his elegant manners—also made her want to hear more regarding this proposal. Instinctively, she felt he was someone she could trust.

She shoved her purse aside and leaned an elbow on the armrest "I'm listening."

"I was on my way to a party. Until my date…"

"I saw the woman leaving this car! I thought she was being left off by a cab. She was your date?"

"Yes, but no longer. We had…"

"A bit of a row?"

"Something like that. Heartbreak." He winced. Heartbreak could only mean they must have broken something off. Poor man. He needed a hug as much as she did.

"I suspect you want to forget your troubles?" he asked.

"I do."

"And while I sympathize for what you've just experienced, I wonder if a little dancing and champagne might lift both of our spirits?"

"I do like champagne. And dancing. And you mentioned tiny hors d'oeuvres?"

"I did indeed. I should not be so bold as to press you to join me. I am a stranger."

"That you are."

He offered his hand for her to shake. "Sebastian Mercier."

The warmth of his hand clasping hers sent a delicious shiver across her shoulders. Her rescuing knight even smelled good, like vanilla and cedar. Azalea had always prided herself on being a good judge of animals. Were they wild, persnickety, trusting or fearful? Judging people was a little hit-or-miss for her. And yet, there was nothing about the man that sent up a warning flag for her. They were comrades in broken hearts.

"Azalea Grace," she said.

"After the flower? It suits you."

"Thanks. My friends call me Lea."

"Would you like to spend a few hours with me in an attempt to forget our troubles? You are dressed for the soiree."

She smoothed a palm over her bespangled skirt. "This dress doesn't belong to me. I'll have to return it. Oh, how do I dare? I can't set foot in that studio again."

"I can see to its return. After the party. You've clothes here?"

She sighed and rifled through the tangled clothing on her lap. "Looks like I only grabbed my jeans during my quick getaway."

"No worries. I will make sure you are properly clothed before the dress is returned. But right now, there's the party."

"I thought it was a soiree?"

"Same thing. Basically. Are you in or out?"

As she let her gaze wander over his face, she exhaled, her shoulders relaxing. Sebastian was not of the same ilk as the man she'd just run from. He was a gentleman. He'd even offered to defend her honor. No man had ever done such a thing. And while she was not so stupid as to be won over by a handsome face and charming manners, the man was also heartbroken and probably felt as rough as she did. What terrible woman had been so cruel to break it off with this gallant knight?

A few hours at a fancy soiree? Her heart leaped before her brain could caution her.

"I'm in," she announced with an effervescent lilt to her tone. "Let's party!"

CHAPTER TWO

AZALEA WASN'T SURE what fantasy world she had entered since plunging into the back of the limo, but she was going along for the ride. Literally. And seated beside a sexy Frenchman wearing an impeccable suit, who kept giving her a smile and a nod? The smolder in his eyes was making parts of her shiver. And in a very good way.

The day had started well. She had been moping over the breakup with Lloyd for weeks, so Maddie had decided to grab her by the fetters and toss her back into life. Before the photo shoot, she and Maddie had done lunch, and then strolled the Jardin du Luxembourg, chatting about their jobs, men and life. Tears had fallen as Azalea had rehashed her recent breakup with Lloyd Cooper. She had genuinely expected him to propose that night at the ritzy restaurant. And to prepare, she'd determined that she must know how he felt about having children before she could answer such a question as a marriage proposal. She'd casually mentioned children over the first course. Lloyd's answer had stunned her. What sort of monster thought children wild and unsuitable for a proper lifestyle?

Then, her heart had crashed. Lloyd had shoved aside his plate and said he couldn't wait one moment longer. He had to confess. He'd hooked up with the woman who owned the flower shop where Azalea worked. The very woman who was also her flatmate! Lloyd had had the audacity to insinuate Azalea was unsophisticated. And she would never fit into his lifestyle, implying that she was a simple farm girl unfit for his important London friends. He and his new lover—her boss!—were headed to Greece the next day for a holiday. They'd insisted Azalea vacate the flat while they were away. So she'd packed her things and trundled home to Ambleside to stay with her dad on the family farm until she could figure out her next step. Finding a new job. And reclaiming her tattered heart.

Why did she always make the wrong choices? If it wasn't a haircut with a seventies-style fluff, it was a horrible spur-of-the-moment lipstick purchase. Why had she thought the eggplant would work against her pale complexion? And had she ever dated a man who hadn't wanted to change her in some way? Even Ralph Madding, the chicken farmer down the road, whom she'd dated when she was nineteen, had complained about her independence. Told her that he required a woman to cook, clean, and have babies with him.

She had nothing against cooking and cleaning. It was the *expectation* of such things that rubbed her the wrong way. Why couldn't men simply exist alongside women and allow them their space while also embracing them? Was that too much to ask?

A night in Paris with a sexy Frenchman she had only met moments earlier? Talk about busting out of her unsophisticated norm! She intended to end this miserable day with a bang.

This dress felt like fairy tissue sprinkled with stardust. The pale pink chiffon floated and was topped overall with a layer of silver-star-bedazzled mesh. Her long, wavy blond hair had been swept up and pinned with sparkling clips to match the stars on the gown. Her makeup was subtle and hadn't succeeded in covering her freckles. And the makeup artist had given her the perfect lip color. Hot pink. Who would have guessed!

Despite growing up on a farm and embracing her inner tomboy, she loved a girlie outfit and the chance to play princess.

She cast a sneaky glance at the seemingly

very kind man who sat next to her on the back seat. He could turn out to be another sleaze. But no, she suspected he wasn't. How many men offered to fight for a woman's honor after knowing her for only a few minutes? She'd be cautious of his smolder, though. Those sexy bedroom eyes and devilishly coiffed dark hair melted bits of her.

She couldn't make two bad choices in one day. The odds must be in her favor!

The car arrived at a fancy building that featured an actual red carpet stretched from curbside and up a flight of stairs to the front doors, where neon lights flashed and music bounced out.

Funny, she'd always thought soirees were more refined, and possibly included tea.

"What kind of party is this?" Now a little nervous, she gripped the door handle. Paris was not her usual stomping ground. She didn't even speak the language. Hobnobbing with an elite crowd was not her style, but a rave or something wild like that would also set her off-kilter.

"A launch bash for Jean-Claude's latest perfume release. It'll be fun."

She liked perfume. And yet. "It looks fancy. Are there celebrities in there?"

Sebastian shrugged. "Probably." When he leaned closer, she inhaled the exotic vanilla and cedar. It tickled at her nerves and softened them. The man was teasingly edible. "I dare you," he offered.

What was it the French declared when taken by something wonderful? *Mon Dieu! Oh, mon Dieu*, this man's eyes. And his smooth baritone voice.

What had he said? Oh, right. He'd *dared* her to go into the party.

Much as whatever waited beyond the red carpet was probably far out of her league, and as unsophisticated as she might be, Azalea wasn't about to be taken down again today. This choice would not blow up in her face. And she wanted to get her mitts all over the promised champagne. And the food. She was hungry! And if opportunity presented, she wouldn't refuse a dance or three.

"Sebastian, right?"

He nodded. "At your beck and call all night, mademoiselle. It'll be fun. Promise."

A promise from a Frenchman wielding a smile that could lure her between the sheets was the most exciting thing she'd ever experienced. She took his hand. And he led her up the red carpet. At the door, a bouncer in dark sunglasses nodded to Sebastian and ticked something on the list he held. If Lloyd could see his little farm girl now!

The ballroom was vast and set in an old building that was tiled, columned, buttressed and everything else one could imagine from ancient architecture. Probably kings and queens had danced across the elaborate marble-tiled floor. The high, curved ceiling featured stained glass Art Deco designs. Mylar streamers, colorful balloons and shimmery fabric hung everywhere. The crowd was dressed to the nines. Diamonds and jewels dazzled.

And… Azalea noticed a lush perfume hanging like an invisible fog over it all. Must be the perfume being launched at the party. It smelled expensive and sweet, like candy.

Then she noticed the word hung overhead, dashed in bold pink neon. *"Câlin?"* she asked.

"It means a hug or something like a cuddle," Sebastian explained. "An odd choice, really, since we French are not keen on hugs. It is the name of the perfume."

"No hugs, eh?"

She imagined wrapping her arms around Sebastian's wide shoulders, fitting her body against his tall figure, and bowing her head against his shoulder, but a kiss away from his alluring mouth. He deserved a hug for rescuing her. As a balm to his own heartbreak. But she didn't want to scare him away—the French weren't keen on hugs?—so she offered up her pinky finger crooked before him.

His quizzical look made her giggle.

"Pinkie hug," she explained. "In honor of the perfume."

He twined his pinkie with hers. Could he contain that smolder that involved a sexy quirk up on one side of his mouth and a soft gaze, or was it a natural movement? "I fear we will both reek of expensive perfume even after leaving."

"It's very nice."

"Smells like something you could eat, yes?"

She nodded her head to the catchy music. "Yes, they must be pumping it into the air. Whew!"

Time to forget her troubles. Forget Lloyd. And the photographer wouldn't be manhandling anything but his private bits for a while. She was here to party.

"Would you like champagne?" Sebastian asked loudly so she could hear over the noise.

"Not yet. I need to dance!"

When she grabbed his hand, he followed her to the center of the ballroom. They insinuated themselves in a spot where they could get their dance on. Three or four songs passed while Azalea's energy soared. Movement always lifted her spirits. The man whom she had literally dragged onto the dance floor showed no signs of wanting to slow down. Undoing the buttons on his suit coat, he countered her moves with some surprisingly rhythmic moves of his own.

When had a man ever matched her silly dance floor energy? Certainly, Lloyd hadn't been able to deflate his pompous upper lip long enough to actually let loose. And despite Sebastian's fancy suit, the diamonds glinting at his cuffs, and what she guessed must be a ridiculously expensive haircut, he danced as if he didn't care what the world thought of him. He'd been dumped by the woman who had fled the back of the limo? Poor guy. They both needed this night.

Grabbing her hand, he twirled her a few times. They developed a dance language with some hip bumping, slides and spins. Azalea laughed and tilted back her head, lifting her arms to become the music.

When the music slowed, she spun and caught her palms against Sebastian's chest. The lights dimmed as the DJ announced a romantic interlude and they swayed beneath the constellation of glimmering party decorations. His cologne tangled with the sweet, perfumed air. Heady and delicious. She inhaled, drawing him into her pores. A girl could lose herself in a moment like this. And maybe she already had.

Something about the enchanting Frenchman

reached inside her and tickled her battered heart. Offered some hope. Even a breathless dare to try again. Might she have a fling with a stranger? It sounded brazen and taboo to her practical heart. But it felt…like something she deserved. A one-night stand? She'd see where the evening led them.

"Are you having a good time?" he asked.

"The best!"

She held up her pinkie and he linked his about hers. "Me as well."

"You're not sorry you're here with someone other than the person you intended to bring here?"

"Not in the least. I've already forgotten her name. You are a spitfire of dance moves and freckles. I could fall in love with you, Azalea Grace."

She laughed, tilting back her head, and he spun her out. Twirling back to hug up against him again, she shook her head and said, "Fall in love all you wish. I would never marry you."

"No worries, my family would never—erm. Why is that?"

His family wouldn't approve of her. That was what he had almost said, but had realized his faux pas. Didn't matter to her. She knew they were not in the same social class. This was just one night. Nothing would spoil it.

She wiggled her shoulders, then shrugged. “Marriage isn’t in the cards for me.” Because—much as she craved a family of her own—she’d been hurt by expecting it to happen. And really? She, married to this fancy, obviously wealthy, man? A ridiculous dream. She must not be crushed twice. Or ever again. “But you know what my next goal is?”

“Do tell.”

“Champagne!”

Hours into the party, Sebastian was on his third glass of champagne, as was Azalea. Lea was what she’d said her friends called her. He’d shortened her name to Zee. He was feeling the alcohol, but not drunk. His senses were sharp and acutely aware of every brush of her skin against his, each sweet smile she cast his way, and her bodacious laugh that seemed to birth from her belly and echo out and spread like the crystal stars suspended over their heads.

This night was multitudes better than he’d expected it to be. And he had expected to be engaged right now.

“Do you know all these people?” she asked as they stood, looking over the dance floor. Somewhere between dances they’d become comfortable with holding hands. It felt as though they’d been holding hands all their lives. "They all seem to recognize you and are so friendly."

"I do know most. It's a tight social circle. My brother was supposed to be here tonight, but I haven't seen him."

Of course, if Philippe had shown he'd have flaunted his latest paramour and inquired why Sebastian was here with an English woman. Not that his family was against the English. It was just that Sebastian tended to date closer to home.

"A Parisian girl will suit you," his mother, Angelique, had a tendency to remind him. *"Not too smart, but beautiful,"* she'd add. *"And don't worry about love, Sebastian. No one marries for love anymore."*

He'd almost blurted that awful statement about his family not approving of her. Uncouth. Yet she hadn't seemed to take it to heart or even notice. *Good save, Sebastian.*

While he hadn't the luxury to waste his time dating a woman of whom his family would never approve, this night wasn't about the competition between himself and Philippe. It was a means to get over tonight's rejection. And apparently, as Zee had spewed out in the limo, she had been rejected recently, too. Her boyfriend hadn't wanted children? And she'd been expecting a proposal?

She was a perfect candidate for Sebastian's

win. He could not have placed an order for a more suitable wife. And he even had a ring in his pocket. But…no. He wasn't so heartless that he could bounce from one woman to the next over the course of a few hours. And he would not take advantage of Zee's broken heart and battered ego after he'd promised her a night of fun.

The live band sang pop songs that spanned decades. When they launched into an eighties' hit, Zee bounced giddily and turned her gleeful eyes to him. He didn't even have to ask.

He took her empty goblet and set it on the bar behind them. "Let's dance!"

Sebastian had never found a woman who liked to dance as much as he did. And who had the energy to keep up with him. Or who couldn't stop worrying about her hair or nails, or her expensive dress, long enough to simply let go and move.

He fit his hands to his surprise date's hips, and they joined a makeshift conga line. What a night! He'd never felt freer. And it was an easy kind of freedom that allowed him to be more intimate with her than he might have thought possible. She didn't mind when he clasped her hand and leaned in close to talk against her ear. She smelled like starlight. And that kind of romantic thinking was what tended to get him into trouble.

This was a one-night adventure. No reason not to enjoy.

After a few songs, he tugged her from the dance floor and to the opposite side of the ballroom. "Did you notice the life-size dioramas?" he asked her. "They're for photographs. Let's do some!"

Staged along the wall were makeshift rooms with props and colorful backgrounds for couples or groups to take fun photos to remember the event. Sebastian strolled toward the first, which featured a setting with paper palm trees. A tropical vacation called to him. A week or so to soak in the sun and forget the demands of work and family.

Suddenly he was jerked to the right.

"This one!" Zee called. "I want to hold the balloons!"

The scene featured a massive bouquet of red balloons set against a cerulean sky background. Zee stepped onto a stepstool and grabbed the balloon strings. Sebastian handed his phone to the assistant that manned each diorama. Then he positioned himself to grasp Zee's legs.

Photo taken, the assistant handed him his phone and Zee bounced up beside him to check the image. It looked as though she were floating away and he was trying to keep her grounded.

"I love it!" she announced, then flitted off again. "I want to do the one with the blossoms!"

Handing his phone to another assistant, Sebastian followed the bouncing woman under a massive paper tree festooned with pink paper flower blossoms. They fluttered everywhere and he had to admit the scene was incredibly romantic. Add to that the perfume that filled his nostrils—and likely all his pores—and he surrendered to the dreamy moment. They took a few shots smiling at the photographer.

Then, she stepped back to take in the overhead blossoms. "This is amazing. So creative."

Sebastian signaled to the assistant she might take a few more shots. He then took Zee's hand and spun her beneath the paper tree. "I'm glad you're having a good time."

"This is a bit of all right! Pinkie hug?"

"Pinkie hug." They linked fingers.

She sighed and tilted her head against his shoulder. Tendrils of her hair had tumbled from the upsweep and she looked tousled but more beautiful for the disarray. The warmth of her body and the press of her breast against his arm lured him to kiss the top of her head.

They met gazes. She smiled and her eyes dropped to his mouth. It felt perfectly natural to kiss her. Softly. Just a brush of his mouth over her pink lips. The sweetness of the moment teased at his emerging desires. When had he shared such a simple yet breathless moment with a woman? Whom he barely knew?

With a tilt of her body, she pressed harder into the kiss and threaded her fingers into his hair, teasing his surprise desires to alert. She tasted of champagne and the too tiny hors d'oeuvres she'd laughed over and then had popped into her mouth between dances. The warmth of her body melded against his as he slid a hand down her back. This dance move was subtle, reading her body, tasting her mouth. She electrified the air and his every desire.

This night could end one of two ways. Delivering her safely to a hotel or…taking her home with him. He knew which of the two he preferred. His inner rogue was not entirely tamable. Nor did he wish to tame it.

And yet something about this woman felt… remarkable. And so different from any woman he'd ever dated.

When suddenly she ended the kiss with a giggle, he turned her in another twirl and then she spun out in search of the next diorama.

The assistant handed back Sebastian's phone to him but muttered as she did so, "I switched to video. Seemed…special." With a wink, the woman turned to accept another phone from a partying couple.

Sebastian sought where his impromptu date had gone. He spied her snagging another tiny treat from a passing silver tray. "She *is* special."

Azalea clutched Sebastian's hand as they wandered along the edge of the dance floor. He'd spoken to so many people, in French, which she didn't understand, but he'd remained cognizant of her presence and those conversations had been short. He would often squeeze her hand and tilt down a smile at her. Gray-blue eyes stood out on his angular face beneath the dark brown, almost black, hair. So sexy. Handsome. A gentleman. A remarkable dance partner. And a hot kisser.

That kiss! What a way to get over a bad breakup. Might Sebastian be considered a rebound guy? Only if they went further than a kiss. And…that was not off the table as far as her desire-filled brain was concerned. A fling might make her feel better about men in general. Boost her confidence. At the very least, she'd leave Paris with a night to remember.

Not that this hadn't already turned into a memorable night. Hand in hand they wandered toward the exit, both in favor of some fresh air. Outside, the warm spring air swirled through her hair and restored her wilting energy.

After texting his driver for a pickup, Sebastian tucked away his phone and slid an arm around her shoulder. She leaned against him as if they were old friends.

Or new lovers. Could she?

Of course, she could. She wasn't that unsophisticated girl Lloyd had so rudely dismissed. Azalea Grace was a beautiful woman who could do anything, and have any man she desired.

"I've never had a better time," he said.

"Same. I sort of wish it wouldn't end."

"It doesn't have to." He saw the limo and waved that he'd seen him. Then he swept Azalea into his embrace.

The kiss was quick, passionate, and it said exactly what she had been considering: *we should take this to the next level.*

"I'm not a hookup kind of guy. But just one night...?"

He held out his hand and she glided hers into it. "Yes, just one night. I want that."

And she did.

CHAPTER THREE

AZALEA OPENED HER eyes to stare upward. The pale morning sky caressed pink-tinged, puffy clouds. With a twist of her head, she could just see the elegant Eiffel Tower in the distance. The two-story-high windows that curved over the bed she lay in captured the top of the city skyline and the dreamy sky. The bed sat on a wooden base, luxurious with sheets that boasted a thread count she was pretty sure exceeded the thousands. An ultrasoft comforter hung to the thick, plush rug spread on the herringbone-patterned wood floor.

Everything smelled like sweet flowers and candy. A hug? What had been the name of that perfume? Câlin. The scent certainly had followed them home. Good thing she liked the smell. But it was all so much.

Sebastian was so much. So much of a good thing.

Sebastian... Sebastian... What was his last name? He'd told her it, but she couldn't recall it.

Azalea suddenly remembered that she wasn't in bed alone. Clutching the sheet to her bare chest, she turned her head. Sebastian lay beside her, his eyes closed, pillow partially over his face and an arm wrapped over the end of it. A strolling gaze traveled from his square jaw with the hint of dark stubble to his broad yet smooth chest that displayed the hard muscles she had traced with her fingers last night. And down to his abs, well-honed and tight. And down farther… Oh, baby, what a night!

Never in her life had Azalea hooked up. Not with a complete stranger. She'd only known the man for hours before following him into bed! Yet from the dancing to the champagne, to the delicious sex, she didn't regret one moment of it. This trip to Paris had turned out to be an uplifting treat after all.

But now the walk of shame. Or rather, the day's journey back to her dad's cottage in Ambleside, where she must finally see to putting her life back together and reenter said life with a plan to move forward. Which entailed…

She didn't know what it entailed. But she did know it was time to stop moping over a failed relationship and get on with it.

Yet the thought of leaving Sebastian's side firmly tugged against the nudge to get up and move on. Maybe a few more minutes lying here, taking it all in.

The man was a dream come true. He ticked all the right boxes, including being a dance phenom, and she did recall at some point he'd offered to defend her honor. She'd loved every minute of the fancy soiree. And the dress had allowed her to easily fit in with the elite crowd. Perhaps being away from home and knowing absolutely no one had allowed her to let loose. Her inner wild child had jumped to the surface. What fun to find a man who enjoyed dancing, being a little silly, and embracing life. They'd pinkie-hugged into one another's lives. Their own secret handshake, of sorts.

Of course, she could have no clue what he thought of last night. Perhaps it was his manner? Hookups might be usual for him. In which case, he might expect to wake and find her gone.

Good plan. She'd gotten what she wanted—a night to remember.

It could never be more than one night. They'd both been burned in a relationship. Last night had been rebound sex. Nothing more. Certainly not if this stylish, big-city man ever learned she was but a simple country girl.

Right. She was out of her league here. Time to shuffle back home.

She carefully slid from the bed to seek out the

bathroom. The spangled dress lay on the floor. Had Sebastian said something about returning it for her? *Yes, please*. She didn't want to face the photographer again. Though he'd been a creep, she had actually stolen a valuable gown from him. She'd leave a note with the name of the studio and trust the dress, along with the heels, would be returned. But that meant she had only her jeans and no shoes or shirt to wear home.

She wandered into a closet whose interior was the length of the bedroom wall. With the ceiling constructed entirely of glass, she could see the elegant suits, shoes and accessories neatly ordered. Each hung exactly two fingers apart. And all colors were arranged by hue in rainbow order. Someone had a bit of fashion OCD. Excusable. She wasn't going to judge a man who had given her, oh, so many orgasms. Had Lloyd even been capable of finding her *on* button? Not without some direction from her. Idiot.

Toward the back of the closet were folded slacks and a couple of neatly folded T-shirts stacked from neutrals to a soft heather tone. She plucked up a black one and held it against her bare chest.

"It'll work."

Grabbing her pants and purse, she slipped into the bathroom and carefully closed the door so as not to wake the sleeping prince who had rescued her from the lecherous villain.

Deciding against a shower because she didn't want to make noise, she splashed some water on her face and borrowed the comb that lay perfectly arranged in the side drawer.

Slipping on her jeans, she then pulled the T-shirt over her head. The scent of Câlin filled her nostrils. She suspected it might have to be sandblasted off her skin. At the very least, it did smell nice. And it reminded her of laughter, dancing and a kiss under pink paper flower blossoms.

Her phone vibrated, and, thankful it wasn't set to ring out loud, she quietly answered when she saw Maddie's name on the screen.

"How'd the photo shoot go?" her friend inquired cheerfully. "Must have been great, because I know what you did last night."

"You...know?" Meaning, the party? The man? The sex? How could she possibly...? "The photo shoot was a bust, Maddie. I had to run—"

"Run? What?"

"The photographer was handsy and a total sleaze. I took off. With the dress. Which I promise I'll return today."

"Oh, my God, Lea, I'm so sorry. I had no idea. I had heard good things about the photographer."

"It's…in the past. I got away from him. And…" Landed in a much more respectful pair of male hands. Who certainly knew how to push all the right buttons on her anatomy. Whew! Surely, that third orgasm had been worthy of her gasping shouts.

"And…" Maddie prompted expectantly.

"Well, you said you knew what I did last night. What did you mean?"

"Câlin," her friend pronounced as if declaring the name of the mysterious fiend on a late-night show.

"How do you…?"

"It's all over social media, Lea."

"You know I don't do social media. What are you talking about?"

"Seems you went to a fancy party last night. A perfume release by Jean-Claude? He's a Parisian icon, Lea. How *did* you manage that invite?"

"Well." Pausing to listen for sound on the other side of the door, Azalea sat on the toilet seat and explained everything from jumping into the limo, to the invite, getting her boogie on, and then landing in bed with the sexy Sebastian. "I'm in his bathroom now."

"OMG! When you get over an ex-boyfriend you really do it right. The photo of you and Sebastian is stunning. He's got you in his embrace and you are laughing. You look so happy. And he is the definition of sexy. Sebastian Mercier." Maddie sighed. "What a catch. But seriously, Lea, you don't want to get involved with that family drama."

Still stuck on his last name—she'd only heard him say it once last night—Azalea wondered why it sounded so familiar.

"Lea, are you listening to me?"

"I am. I wonder what photo that was?" From one of the diorama shots? Though, she did recall some shots taken in the crowd. Sebastian had slid an arm about her waist and leaned in to pose for a number of people. Had one of them been a reporter? "Why does his last name sound familiar?"

"L'Homme Mercier? Remember, Lea, we rented tuxes from them last year for my wedding?"

"Wow—the most famous menswear designer in Paris?"

"Yes, dearest, *that* Mercier family. They own an elite atelier in the sixth and another shop in the Place des Vosges. And, apparently, you are not aware of what the poster wrote about that family's current competition."

"Competition? I don't understand any of this, Maddie. And I'm hungry. I need eggs and toast.

With beans and tomatoes and a few of those curly onion bits sprinkled—"

"Lea! Focus. Listen to me."

Visions of steaming eggs set aside, Azalea nodded. "Right. Fill me in."

"So apparently your sexy dance partner and his brother are in a competition to win the CEO position of the family company. The first brother to marry and produce an heir wins."

Azalea's jaw dropped. Her sweet, sexy lover who could dance her into dreams both on the dance floor and in between the sheets was… looking for a wife? And an heir? As part of a competition.

Suddenly she wished for a toothbrush because the bad taste in her mouth stunk.

"That doesn't…" Sound like the man who had saved her last night. And had given her a taste of real, delicious passion.

But she knew nothing about him. So, he loved to dance. And make love. And was kind. An actual rescuer of lost, makeshift princesses. But had such amiable heroics been a ruse? The woman who had dashed away from the limo—Had he been trolling for a wife last night?

"Lea? Talk to me."

"I…thanks for telling me that, Maddie." This was a lot to process. "But don't worry about me.

It was just a hookup. I'm not in the market for a husband. You know marriage is not on my list."

"Is that so? It was on your list. Your goal of having kids and raising them wild and feral on a farm isn't going to happen without a man, Lea."

"That goal can be attained. Doesn't mean the participating man has to be my husband." Oh, how she lied to herself!

Maddie sighed. "Sebastian Mercier is worth millions."

"So? I'd never marry a man just because he's got money. You know me better than that."

"I do. And I believe that sweet, quirky Lea landed in the arms of a millionaire by accident and was swept away on a fantasy night of dancing and passion. And you know what? You deserve it. A night on the town. Doing as you please. With whomever you please. But it's a new day. What are you going to do now?"

"I'm heading home. I had my fun." And had made another wrong choice! Just when she'd thought she'd turned a corner on her bad decisions. Argh! "Time to get back to my life."

"Which means…? Are you going to find work in London and rent a new flat?"

"Well." Staying at her parents' farm provided a convenient hideaway from the real world.

"Lea. Don't let Lloyd's rejection bring you down any longer. You're better than that. And you don't have to go back to that flower shop. Find a new shop that's not owned by a backstabbing, boyfriend-stealing witch. You'll find something."

"I know I will." Pausing to listen for sound on the other side of the door, she was reassured by the silence. "I gotta go, Maddie. I want to duck out of here before he wakes."

"Oh, baby, you've had a night. Just don't trip and land in his arms again. That man could prove a real problem."

"No kidding. I'm not that stupid. At least, I'm not going to be that stupid about a man anymore."

"Hallelujah!"

"Talk later, Maddie."

She hung up and stuffed the phone in her purse. Then she faced the woman in the mirror. Hair tousled but still a bit wavy from the updo. She shook her head and exhaled.

"It was a fun night." No way would she deny herself that win. "But you need to dash before you do land in his arms again."

Because Maddie knew she had a weakness for a sexy man with pleading eyes and a heroic heart. What woman would not? But apparently this sexy man needed a wife and child. To consider such a fulfilling prospect—no. This wasn't her world. Azalea Grace loved her small life. It made her happy. Besides, a relationship with

Sebastian would lead nowhere. How could it? He had a wife to find. A company to win! Better to walk away with her heart intact while the walking was possible.

With a firm jut of her chin, Azalea pulled on her metaphorical big-girl knickers—because in reality she was sans knickers—and snuck out of the best thing that would never happen to her.

Sebastian pulled up a pair of soft, jogging slacks and called out to Azalea. He assumed she was in the bathroom, though he didn't hear any running water. He raked his fingers through his hair.

The petite bit of freckles and blond hair had rocked his world last night.

They had danced like no one was watching. Laughed until his jaw had ached. Had sex, Really amazing sex. They needed to do all of the above again. Before she left and returned for home.

"Zee?" He wandered over to the bathroom door and rapped with his knuckle. A twist of the knob, and he slowly opened the door... "Zee?" He scanned the penthouse behind him, not seeing any sign of her.

His gaze landed on the dress folded neatly on the vanity. The shoes were placed next to it, along with a note written on a piece of cardboard torn from a soap box.

Sebastian, it was an amazing night. I'll never forget it! Saw social media this morning. You're in a competition with your brother? Time for me to leave. Only good memories. Promise. You said you'd return the dress for me. Here's the address...

Sebastian cursed under his breath. She'd learned about the competition on social media? He rushed out to the bedroom and grabbed his phone to open the one social media app he used and searched for his name. A photo of him embracing a laughing Azalea popped up.

"So gorgeous," he whispered. "And happy."

And yet, after the night they'd had together she'd decided to sneak out without saying goodbye? Would she have waited and spent some time with him had she not seen the post? He would never know.

Sebastian looked out the window and ran his fingers through his hair. Had the best thing that had ever happened to him just slipped away?

No, it had been a one-night fling. In a few days he'd forget all about Azalea Grace. And her cute freckles. And her bubbly presence. And her delicious and surprisingly commanding kisses. Life would move forward. Back to the wife hunt.

He turned his phone over to peer at the social media post. Her smile was so effusive. Her entire face squinched and her eyes closed, drawing all attention to those remarkable freckles. He could hear her laughter even now and smell...well. *Mon Dieu,* that perfume had followed them home. They'd literally danced it into their systems. Despite its pleasantness, a long shower was in order.

Before tossing his phone to the bed, he recalled they'd taken some shots in interactive stages featured around the ballroom. Flicking through his camera files, he found the photos. In one, Azalea grasped a bouquet of balloons and stood on a concealed stool that made it look as though she were floating upward. Arms wrapped around her waist, he appeared to bring her back down as he looked up adoringly at her.

Sebastian smiled. Tapped the photo until it wobbled with a trash can on the corner of the photo. And then...he shook his head.

"No, I don't want to forget you."

CHAPTER FOUR

WITH THE SUN setting soon, Azalea found her bicycle parked behind the bookstore where she'd left it yesterday morning before catching a train to London to make the trip to Paris. She knew the store owner and had gotten permission years ago to use the rack. Everyone in Ambleside knew everyone else. It was a tourist town renowned for its hiking trails and beautiful scenery. It was one of many small towns in the Lake District that sat upon Lake Windermere.

Her dad, Oliver Grace, had texted her around noon. He and his girlfriend had left to catch their afternoon flight out of London to Australia. Would she be home soon to tend Stella? Yes, not to worry.

The bike ride was a pleasant meander along the paved roads and cobbled Ambleside streets to country lanes lined with mown grass and bright yellow buttercup and pale pink thrift. Inhaling the fresh air, she allowed the remaining sunshine to beam through her pores, reviving her muscles after the tedious hours of travel. Still, the perfume lingered on her. Most likely she'd left a scent trail on all the trains she taken from Paris to home.

One night in Paris? Well spent when she considered her sexual needs had been met. Big-time.

It was that pinkie hug from Paris that she needed to forget. And that smolder. The man was in a competition that required him to find a wife and have a child? Might Azalea Grace ever manage to pick a normal man?

Apparently, she was not meant to find a happily-ever-after sort of guy. At least, not the sort who could meet her expectations of what she wanted in her future. Country cottages and barefoot children, anyone? Yes, please. She'd meant it when she'd told Maddie marriage was off the table.

Maybe.

Dash it, her heart knew that was a lie. Her idea of the perfect life did involve marriage, and not living on her own, children or no children. But she would not marry a man simply because he'd rocked her world and needed her to win a competition.

"Forget about him," she muttered to her pining heart.

Once at the cottage, set in a dip beyond a sharp right turn and but a stone's throw from the lake, she parked her bike against the weather-bleached fence that had once kept wild rabbits from the garden but now tended to merely entice them to try their hand—or rather, paw—at wiggling through the wide gaps between slats.

She wandered into the cozy, brick-and-stone, nineteenth-century farmhouse that had been completely renovated two decades ago. In the kitchen, she filled a water bottle and walked out to the creaky yet comforting porch, where she sat on the steps overlooking a tidy and currently rabbit-less yard. Sunlight glittered on the wildflowers to her right and on the pond surface where a couple of wild ducks floated.

After a day filled with abrupt naps and rude awakenings—she could never sit on a train and not fall asleep within minutes—finally she had a moment to breathe.

She kicked off the cheap trainers she'd purchased at a tourist shop before hopping a train at the Gare du Nord and leaned against the porch railing. The wood was worn and smooth at her back because this was where she had sat all her life.

And soon it would be no more.

Her dad intended to sell the farm and cottage. Grace Farm had taken in and rehabilitated animals for almost three decades. Oliver Grace had started it along with Azalea's mother, Petunia.

Now her dad wanted a new adventure. Which he had gotten with his girlfriend, Diane, a woman who defined the term *wanderlust* with a sparkle in her eye and occasional bits of grass in her hair and personal possessions proudly confined to but a rucksack.

Azalea was happy that her dad was moving on after her mother had divorced him three years earlier. Petunia Grace had told Azalea she felt confined. Needed to be free. It had been as amicable an ending as a thirty-year relationship could be. Her mom had moved to Arizona to start a crystal business with a longtime friend. A male friend who had read Petunia's aura and declared them soul mates.

So that was how freedom looked? Apparently.

The divorce had finally forced Azalea to move to London. Yes, she hadn't left home until she was twenty-two, being perfectly content to live on the farm and have no aspirations or ambitions other than to breathe fresh air and befriend any animal the farm took in.

London hadn't been so much a rude awakening as merely a much-needed rousing. Azalea had discovered a world beyond the confines of the country, and she'd enjoyed most of it. She'd stayed a few weeks with her sister, Dahlia, a lawyer. Dahlia had left the farm at sixteen, never to look back, compelled by the beck of the busy city and all its opportunities. She'd helped Azalea find a flat and a lovely job as flower arranger for a tiny shop tucked between a bookstore and a vinyl record shop. It had suited her. She had been happy. Much as Dahlia gently prodded her to aspire for something higher, more fulfilling, Azalea had never felt the need to enter the corporate rat race. She preferred a simple life, with simple things.

And though a tomboy at heart, she did have aspirations to become a princess. That childhood fantasy still held space in her heart. Not real royalty, but rather, well…last night had contributed to the fantasy. Fabulous gown, pretty makeup and shoes, an elite event filled with stardust and champagne. And a handsome knight.

Azalea inhaled the perfume that coated her skin and which had even imbued the T- shirt she wore. *His shirt.* She wished it smelled like him—sultry vanilla and cedar—but no such luck. A lovely parting gift to remember her one night in Paris?

Last night's fling had been amazing. Not a thing to complain about when viewing the larger picture. Sebastian had been perfect. Handsome. Kind. Fun. Even a little silly when they'd been dancing up a storm. An excellent lover. Obviously rich. But apparently in the market for an instant wife so he could gain control of the family company. That pesky detail could not be dismissed.

And he hadn't considered *her* a possible wife? He'd started to say something about his family not approving, but she'd forced herself to ignore it at the time. She had a right to be miffed at that exclusion. Even if it felt as if she'd dodged a bullet. So, like she'd written to him, she would remember the night, cherish it, but it was time to move on. More wrong choices to make, don't ya know?

A sneaky little devil landed on her shoulder and prodded her in the heart.

You liked him. A lot. Don't act like you wouldn't jump if you saw him again.

She sighed, catching her chin against her palm. Her heart did have a tendency to leap before her brain could stop her. Here she sat in a little piece of heaven on earth, undisturbed by the rush of the real world, and still Sebastian Mercier haunted her thoughts.

There was one problem. She hadn't given him her phone number and she'd not gotten his contact info. Though certainly she did know where he worked. L'Homme Mercier was a well-known Parisian brand. Maddie had mentioned the two ateliers. A quick browse online could easily locate them. She could make contact.

Yet, that felt like diving into something she

wasn't sure was good for her. If he wanted to see her again, he'd find her.

And if she never saw him again, she'd have to accept that was how it was meant to be. Obviously, the man had a wife to catch. And she was all about not becoming a wife now.

Azalea sighed. Her relationship with Lloyd had broken her in a surprising manner. And one night with a stranger hadn't been able to pry the memory from her brain cells. Because of that breakup she'd developed a healthy fear of commitment. Marriage? Once it had been all she'd desired. Until Lloyd had reduced it to a condition of social status, and Sebastian had further cemented it with his emotionless quest for a wife. And while her parents had shown her that anything could be broken and still survive, she didn't want to touch the idea of an extended attachment with someone she didn't love or a man she might even eventually fall out of love with.

Yet her romantic heart still wanted love and a relationship. She wanted to be cherished, admired, and be a friend and lover. She wanted to be a mother.

Well. Wasn't as if Sebastian had intended to propose to her anyway.

Which left her here. Alone and unsure what her future held.

A moo from the barn clued her it was feeding time. Her dad, a bovine veterinarian, had taken in injured or sick cows for decades. He cared for them, tended their injuries and nursed them back to health before they were either returned to their owner or, if abandoned, lived in happiness on the lush acres of Grace Farm. Stella, a highland cow with a long brown coat and pearly white hooves, had given birth to a calf two months earlier. The little one was so fluffy it looked like a walking plushy. Her dad hadn't named the newborn, insisting he didn't want a reason to get attached when his plans involved selling them both before summer's end. In the few weeks Azalea had been staying here, she and the cow had become best of friends.

Stella wandered toward the wooden fence attached to the side of the barn and Azalea stepped down onto the grass in her bare feet.

"Stella!" she called. "You'll never believe the night I've had."

In a quiet office on the top floor of a 6th arrondissement building the Mercier family had owned for over a century, Sebastian leaned back in his chair. Two stories below, the atelier created bespoke suits for an elite clientele. The shop on the Place des Vosges carried their prêt-à-porter collection. Both shops drew clients worldwide.

L'Homme Mercier had begun in the 1920s as a tailor shop set up by Sebastian's great-great-grandfather and had grown exponentially over the years. It was a Paris icon. Their clients were rich and many. Yet the company prided itself on individual attention and exquisite detail to every piece of clothing it produced. Never mass-scale production. And marketing was tasteful yet sensual.

Philippe's suggestion that they integrate women's wear into their *oeuvre* was unthinkable. But his brother, just down the hall in his office, was moving ahead with plans, designs and clothing sketches. While their father, Roman, had not approved of the idea, neither had he rejected Philippe's ruse. That glint in Roman Mercier's eyes always indicated that he had set the parameters for the future of L'Homme Mercier. And those parameters would be controlled by whichever son first married and produced an heir.

A competition declared just weeks after Roman had suffered a stroke. It had only put him in the hospital overnight. The doctor had said Roman was very lucky in that his girlfriend had recognized the signs—one side of his face had drooped and he'd not been able to get his words out—and had immediately taken him to the emergency room. But that little brush with mortality had set Roman on a quest to secure his legacy.

Sebastian had never viewed the competition as silly or unthoughtful. Or even out of character for his father. It was what he knew. All his life he and Philippe had competed, be it on the lacrosse field, or attracting *Le Monde* for a feature article, or at boat racing at Marseilles. They earned their worth through their father's nod of approval.

And while this new competition would involve another person—and *creating* another person—his child—Sebastian set his heart to it as with all other competitions. And this time he must win. L'Homme Mercier would not be diluted by mass marketing and—by all the gods—a women's clothing division.

Did the battle require he be in love? Not at all. In fact, the idea of love equating to marriage was not a Mercier philosophy. Roman Mercier had four sons. By three different mothers. He'd never married any of the women. And while Sebastian knew there was something not quite right with that family structure, he also knew nothing else. Which did make the marriage stipulation a little strange.

Why did Roman insist on signed legal papers? Shouldn't an heir be enough? And really, was Sebastian supposed to put some woman's name on a piece of official paper that granted her half of everything he owned? That did not sit well with him. So he'd be sure to have a prenup drawn up.

Sebastian was very capable of taking control of the family legacy. He knew the company from bottom to top. He'd started in the sewing department when he was thirteen, learning the trade and taking pride in the occasional nod of approval from the tailors. Later, he'd moved up to promotions and design, and now he was in charge of the finances, shipping and suppliers. As well as sharing marketing duties with Philippe. Just last week he'd worked men's fashion week, which was held annually in Paris. It was always a whirlwind of fashion, celebrities, news media, interviews, parties and pressing flesh with all the right people. Philippe had missed half of it because he'd been in Marseilles schmoozing with an Austrian royal of the female persuasion. So, who was *really* devoted to the company?

Yet, during that exhausting week of fashion shows, Sebastian had struggled with distracting thoughts of *her*. Azalea Grace of the freckles and bubbly laughter. A woman who had leaped into his life, swirled him dizzy on the dance floor, and then dashed out as quickly.

But not without a pinkie hug. He smiled to think about that little gesture they'd developed between them within the short period they'd been together. The woman had dug up his fun side and he'd reveled in it. He hadn't felt so exhilarated and unguarded since he was a child. It was almost as if he'd been swept away into a fairy tale. Silly to think like that. Though she had mentioned something about feeling like a princess. And hadn't he been her rescuing knight?

A tilt of his head confirmed that bemusing thought. And yet. It had ended abruptly. Didn't feel right, either. Like Zee had left behind a hole in him with her sneaky departure. And that hole needed to be—well, he wasn't sure. Was it that he merely lusted after her? Or was there something more? The affection she'd given him so easily had felt genuine and surprisingly new. She hadn't asked for a thing in return, save another dance.

Had he seriously not gotten her contact info? Stupid of him. All he knew was her name and that she lived in England. Some village, or tourist town called Bumblebush. Or Anglewood. Or...he couldn't recall. He must remember the name. Because he wanted to see her again. Even as he'd schmoozed and shaken hands with the press and talked to all sorts at cocktail parties last week, whenever a beautiful woman had caught his eye, he'd looked away. Thought of Zee's springy blond hair. Those bright blue eyes that had reflected joy. And so many freckles.

And that kiss under the paper cherry blossoms. He'd watched the video of it every evening, remembering the softness of her skin, the warmth of her sigh, the utter indulgence of her body melting against his. She'd gotten under his skin. Even more so than that blasted perfume.

Such nostalgic longing wasn't like him. Sebastian Mercier was a playboy. Just like his father. He loved women. Had found the process of frequent dating in his search for the perfect wife not at all taxing. And yet, for some reason, he hadn't hooked up with a single woman since the night of the perfume debut party. Quite out of character for him.

He toggled the mouse to bring his computer screen awake and decided to search for the name of the English village. If he could figure that part out, it shouldn't be too difficult to then find a woman named Azalea. He did have the photos of them from the party. He wondered if he could search for her that way. Might bring up a social media page?

His phone rang and, just when he thought to ignore it, a text popped up from his brother at the same time. Curious.

Sebastian answered the call, which was also Philippe, "What is it?"

"It's Dad. He's had another stroke."

CHAPTER FIVE

Months later

So MUCH HAD happened as summer swelled. And so much had stayed the same.

Azalea's dad had called during week six of his vacation asking her if she wouldn't mind keeping an eye on things a bit longer. A few more weeks? Of course, that was no problem, she'd reassured him. And it wasn't. She loved the farm. She and Stella were best friends. And the half dozen chickens weren't too much trouble, save for Big Bruce, the cockerel, who had a habit of scampering off to the neighbor's farm and—well, she'd gotten more than a few rude phone calls pleading her to keep her cock locked up.

She'd gotten over the breakup with Lloyd. His loss. And with his lack of empathy, he would have never made a good father to her future children. Because, yes, children were her future.

And yet, the one thing that had altered in

Azalea's heart lately was her need for companionship. It was more an inner blooming that pressed her to figure out her life. And to do it quickly.

Would she remain on this farm forever? No. It would go up for sale as soon as her dad returned. But where would she go and what would she do? London had been fine, but it had never felt like her place. Like a forever home. It was too busy. Too crowded. Too…just, too.

Even more, now she sought stability and comfort. Protection, even. In a sort of "man wrapping his arms around her and keeping her close" manner. Had she blown it by walking out of Sebastian Mercier's life?

She shook her head. Even if they had continued to see one another, she could have never been assured he wasn't using her simply for the wife and child stipulation that would have won him the CEO position.

Yet still, she was frustrated.

"Things have gotten complicated." She swore a bit more loudly than usual. Sometimes a well-intoned oath was required.

"Stella…" Azalea swept hay from the barn floor while the cow watched through the open gate at the end of the breezeway. "You and Daisy seem to get along well on your own." She'd named the calf. Difficult to keep calling her *lit-*

tle one. And the little plushy did enjoy nibbling daisies in the field. "You think I can manage?"

The cow rubbed her cheek against the worn door frame, a favorite place to scratch.

"I am very capable of living on my own," she defended to no one but herself. Taking care of her own, she thought with a proud lift of her chest. "And I will find a job. I enjoy arranging flowers. There's a florist in Ambleside next to the ice cream parlor."

Yet it might never pay enough to ensure even the simple lifestyle she desired. She needed to get serious and figure out a means to an income to support herself.

Having been content on the farm for such a long time, she'd never considered pursuing higher education to enable her to get a nine-to-five job. Dahlia was the go-getter, the woman with a plan and a target. That target being becoming partner in her law firm and a million-pound home in Notting Hill. Dahlia knew her little sister was not so financially ambitious and had never tried to provoke her toward something beyond what she aspired to. Yet, Azalea was well aware she'd become complacent. Set in her ways.

Her parents' divorce had shaken her out of that complacence. Once located in London, she'd realized the only jobs she was qualified for were fast-food slinger—ugh; hotel maid—she did not like touching other people's messes; rubbish collector—seriously?—or simple yet creative jobs that she could easily learn, such as floral arranging. She didn't regret not furthering her education. The world was filled with self-starters, independent minds who made their own way. She just needed to make some life changes. Focus on her strengths. And…sooner, rather than later.

Because she'd taken a pregnancy test twice now. Both times it had confirmed the new life growing inside her. She'd only smiled about it since. Not once had she felt regret.

Honestly? Very well, anxiety had struck. And tended to wake her in the middle of the night. Could she do this? Could she actually be a mother? And do it alone?

What about Sebastian? He was the father, no doubts on that one. Should she include him? Did she want him in her life once the baby was born? Of course, the father should be allowed that option. But what if he insisted she marry him? He did, after all, outweigh her when it came to power, influence, and having access to hard-hitting lawyers. She barely knew the man. Might she risk getting trapped in his competitive plans for marriage? Plans that did not include love.

"Love is important," she muttered.

Stella mooed, as if in agreement.

"Exactly." She hung up the broom and slapped her palms across her khakis to disperse the hay dust. "I don't think I can tell him."

Stella's next moo was more admonishing. Azalea had debated with her nearly every evening when she went to muck out the stable. Should she or shouldn't she tell Sebastian?

Yet another moo and a curt dismissal as Stella turned to find Daisy. The cow left Azalea standing there with her hands on her hips. And her heart begging to be included in the debate.

"But there's no way to tell him," she insisted.

Another lie she told her heart. She'd already marked the GPS location of L'Homme Mercier on her phone. Flying to Paris and showing up at the atelier to announce Sebastian was going to be a father was not an impossibility.

"I don't know. I just...don't know how to do it in a reasonable and nonconfrontational manner. There will be a row. Loud words. Accusations. Questions. So many questions, surely. I've got enough to deal with in figuring out this pregnancy thing."

Put her indecision down to hormones.

Then she reprimanded herself for having normal doubts any new mother must experience. She was thrilled over being pregnant. Having a baby as a single woman hadn't been a choice she'd made in the moment. She and Sebastian had used protection. What was it she'd heard about a condom's failure rate? Something like two percent? She wouldn't even label it wrong. This baby felt right.

With or without Sebastian.

Wandering outside, she nearly slipped in the mud that curled around the barn but caught herself with a swing of her hand just dipping into that muck.

Swiping a palm over her thigh, she lifted one foot, clad in a mud-coated wellie, and the suction released her. Farm life. If she didn't end the day with mud, straw or some unidentifiable substance stuck to her hair, skin or clothing, it just wasn't a day.

"I'm going to shower, then take a walk in the field to collect some cornflowers for a bouquet," she told Stella. "You and Daisy might join me if you care to. Be back in a bit."

She strode to the back of the cottage, where a makeshift, outdoor shower fitted over a stone mat was useful for clearing away the mud. But before she could turn on the spigot, she heard a car. Driving *away* from the cottage? The property was in a neat little private area, sporting a long drive lined with hedgerows. Had someone been up to the front without her knowing? Possible. When in the barn it was difficult to hear beyond the back of the cottage. She wasn't expecting any deliveries.

Swinging around the side of the cottage, Azalea dodged the overgrown vines that she swore she'd tend soon and pushed open the creaky iron gate. A man stood on the fieldstone pathway curling to the front door. A smart black suitcase sat on the ground beside him. He was quite well-dressed. In a stunning suit—

Azalea swore under her breath. In an instant her heartbeat went from calm to freakout. She patted her frazzled hair, which she might or might not have combed this morning.

At the sight of her, he waved. Even at this distance his smile danced into her heart and giddied in her belly. He'd seen her! No chance to duck away and hide. To fix her hair. To—she studied her dirty hands—yikes, did she have mud in her hair, too?

How had he found her? Why was the sexiest man in Paris standing before her cottage with a smile that shouldn't be there if he could get a good look at her?

"Zee!"

He could call her all he liked, but that didn't make her feet move forward. She was frozen in shock. And not because she must look a fright.

Well, yes, there was that. But because—her hand went to her belly.

"Sebastian," she said on a gasp.

She'd gone over this moment many a time with Stella. How to tell him? *Should* she tell him? The answers depended on whether she'd see him again. And now here he was. Standing in her front yard. And she had not practiced for this scenario.

Seeing her frozen there, dumbstruck, Sebastian stepped carefully on the overgrown grass, and beelined around a crop of fieldstones that were supposed to be yard decoration but really her dad had tossed there because he didn't want to haul them to the back of the property.

When he stood before her, Azalea still felt like a statue that could barely breathe. Her insides were rushing, gushing and flip-flopping all at once. And the little tyke growing inside her had many months before it began to move about, so she knew it was nerves.

"I found you," he announced. "And believe me, it wasn't easy. But once I figured out that you lived in Ambleside, all I had to do was go around with your photo and ask—"

"You have my photo?" she dumbly blurted.

"Yes." He tugged out his phone and turned the screen toward her. The screensaver showed them in that silly pose they'd taken at the party with her flying away, balloons in hand, and him grasping to pull her down. "Everyone had a good laugh at the photo. They all knew it was you and where you lived. Though I must admit, finding a place 'just beyond the dip' was an interesting excursion."

"Yes, the dip in the road."

She gestured toward the road, realizing it was stupid to even converse about the condition of the old, winding road when the man of her dreams stood before her. Looking like a god who could conquer all of womankind with his smolder and a tug at his perfectly fitted suit. And she looking like the one who got trampled on by the masses as they rushed him for his favor.

"I'm sorry it took so long to come see you," he said. "I've thought about you every day."

"Same," she whispered more softly than her heart screamed. She must tell him.

Oh, heart, be quiet!

"After you left Paris, I was busy with fashion week. Which takes up a few weeks businesswise. And then my father had a stroke. Another one, actually. It was difficult to get away."

"Oh, dear, Sebastian, your dad? Is he all right?"

"Yes, he's recovering and dealing with some speech issues now. The old man needs to slow down. Take things easy."

And insist one of his sons get married and have a child so they could take control of the company? The thought shoved Azalea like a bully with his hands to her back, but she swallowed down a yelp, or worse, an oath.

"Is it all right that I've come?" he asked.

He took her in, his eyes gliding over her. Gray-blue irises caught the sunlight and toyed with her sense of personal space. Her newly acquired need to protect her growing family at all costs. And yet, all she wanted was to claim a hug from the man who had explained that the French simply didn't do that.

"You don't look pleased to see me."

Azalea exhaled and shook her head. "I am pleased. I think. I mean, well, it is a surprise, isn't it? I hadn't thought to see you again. Though...yes, I am pleased. Well. I feel a bit mussed right now. Been mucking out the barn. Would you like to come inside while I refresh?"

"I'd love to."

Sebastian had risked rejection jetting off to London, then on to the little village of Ambleside without having a means to notify Zee he was on his way. He'd gone from a café to a pub and, photo of Azalea displayed on his phone, had gotten lucky at the second stop. A young man around Azalea's age knew her from school and had directed Sebastian to take the west road for a distance, then turn right after the dip.

Surprisingly, the driver had found the place.

Now he sat at a round table graced with a bouquet of wilting blue flowers. The house was small and epitomized cottage core, with the checked curtains, cozy rugs, low ceilings and tidy cupboards. He heard a cow moo in the distance and the occasional crow of what he guessed could be a cockerel. That night at the party he'd guessed she wasn't of his world, but he'd not expected an actual farm girl. He was not put off but he also wasn't sure what to expect. He'd only ever dated city girls, women who'd given a care for their hair, nails and always the perfect outfit.

What sort of travesty had been those rubber boots covered in mud? And even more mud in her hair and on her face?

And yet, at the sight of Azalea—his Zee—his heart had bounced. Almost like a dance he'd shared with her at the party. He'd found her. The woman who had jumped into his life and as quickly jumped out of it.

He'd had to make this trip. He wanted to get to know her. To see if this compulsion to find her was something more. But also, since his father's second stroke, the pressure to win the competition and take control of the company had increased. The risk that his father might have another stroke was high. And he might not survive the next one. L'Homme Mercier must be put in order before then, with the long-established traditions firmly in place without threat of change.

And if Zee had been on his mind so much, then, Sebastian had reasoned, perhaps he should entertain the idea of making *her* his wife? They both got along. And she had mentioned something about wanting a family and children. He'd come here to learn if she might be amenable to the idea. But even more so, he wanted to learn if he still felt the same way toward her. If they spent the night squabbling or couldn't find a common interest, then he'd mark the trip off as closing the door on a wonder that had prodded at his heart for months. On to the next potential wife. It was something he had to do for the company.

"Sorry to keep you waiting," she announced as she sailed down a curved stairway hugging a stone wall. "I didn't realize how much mud I had on me. It's Stella's fault."

"Stella being…?"

"Uh…my best friend."

The crinkle of her brow was so cute. Everything about her, from the tips of her now bare toes, up to her freckled knees, and the simple green checked dress to her button nose and more freckles on her checks. Her hair was fluffed and a little wet, and those bright eyes. The woman was simply stunning.

"So you found me." She stood at the base of the stairs, hands fidgeting before her.

Approaching her, unsure if she would allow it, Sebastian watched for a panicked look but only got a stunned blink of her eyes. Damn it, he'd been dreaming about this reunion for weeks. And it always started with a kiss. So he kissed her. And, thankfully, she didn't resist.

It had been too long. He'd thought about her kisses, her bare skin, the warmth of her body gliding against his. Her sweet murmurs as they'd made love that night, over and over. How the moonlight had glowed like pearls over her naked body. The two of them smelling like that crazy perfume and giggling about it. Now she was back in his arms. And a sweet murmur reassured him he was not overstepping any lines.

Something about holding Azalea Grace felt… fragile. Yet also a greedy desire prodded at him. He wanted the thing he wasn't supposed to have. And the little boy in him wouldn't allow any others to take it away from him.

When he pulled away to study her reaction, she nodded and said, "Yep, not a mistake."

"What's a mistake?"

"Nothing's a mistake. I was just remembering our night in Paris. It wasn't a mistake. That kiss reminded me of how real and fun it was."

"It was fun. And real. But too quick." He held up his hand, pinkie finger extended.

She twined hers with his. "Yes, too—well!" She quickly disengaged. "Now that you've found me, you must realize that I am a farm girl. Definitely not the type you're accustomed to dating. I'm not sure why you'd even bother coming to see me."

"Zee, I can't look at another woman without comparing her to you. I had to find you to see if the feeling I get every time I think of you was real. And well, it is real. I'm feeling those same flutters. Hell, it's like an animal pull to hold you, touch you, make love to you all over again. And I don't care if you're a farm girl."

"Yes, you do."

He shrugged, then chuckled. "There are certain odors out here, aren't there?"

She laughed. "But not me, I hope?"

"No, you smell like summer."

"And you…" She sniffed and then crinkled her freckled nose. "Do you smell of Câlin?"

"That perfume seems to have gotten into every fiber of clothing in my closet. I thought I'd aired it out but apparently not."

"That's crazy." She strolled to the sink, flicked

on the faucet and grabbed a glass. Distancing herself from him? Not a good start.

"I wish you hadn't left without kissing me goodbye. But I understand. I'm sorry you had to find out about the competition from social media."

"I had to sneak out. I wasn't prepared to do the morning-after awkwardness. And the competition means nothing to me since we're not even a thing."

"We could be a thing."

"Listen, I'm not a fool, Sebastian. I'm so out of your social echelon."

"Oh, we're talking echelons now? Those are fighting words."

She laughed over a sip of water. "Be serious, Sebastian. You asked that woman to marry you. She fled. You didn't ask me to marry you because I do recall you saying your family would never approve."

He should have never let that slip! "Do you want me to ask you? I recall you saying you'd never marry me."

"You got that right."

He clutched the back of a chair before the table. He hadn't expected this to be easy. "Still don't understand why this visit bothers you."

"It's just that, why waste your time on me? Surely you and your brother are in a race to win the prize. And with your father—oh, I'm sorry. I shouldn't make assumptions regarding his health."

"Assume anything you like. Philippe and I *are* in a race since Father's second stroke. It affected him more this time around. He can no longer go into the office. I've had to take over dealings with his special client list and Philippe has been traveling nonstop. We..." He shoved a hand over his hair and splayed it out before him. "Zee, can this just be what it is? I had to see you again."

"So you've seen me." She crossed her arms.

Not going to give him an inch? What had he done to make her so...disinterested? He'd thought they had parted on common ground, both quite pleased with their time spent together. Although she must've been miffed to learn about the competition. He'd give her that.

"Give me twenty-four hours," he challenged.

"What for?"

"To talk to you, get to know you." Find that crazy, silly happiness they'd shared with one another when they sailed around the dance floor. "I just want to be with you, Zee."

"Have sex with me, is what you mean."

"That would be ideal, but it's not a requirement."

She shook her head, then spread a palm over her stomach. "I don't know."

"You don't want to entertain a visitor for a while? Come on, Zee, give me a chance. Show me around. Take me into town. Introduce me to Stella. Can you tell me you haven't thought of me once since fleeing my home?"

"I didn't flee."

"You exited without saying goodbye, which is the definition of fleeing."

"Fine, I fled. And…very well. I'm not hating you being here in my home. My dad's home. I'm just watching the place until he returns from vacation."

"Tell me about it."

"Seriously?"

He spread out his arms. "You can't get rid of me now. I sent the driver away."

It took a while for her smile to blossom, but when it did her nose wiggled and her eyes brightened even more. She was so adorable. And he had just won the next twenty-four hours with her.

CHAPTER SIX

AZALEA OFFERED TO make a light meal, so a salad it was. Everything was fresh from the garden or field, even the mustard seed dressing. She and Sebastian sat out back on the porch, plates on their laps, wineglasses close to hand. Of course, she only had cherry-flavored sparkling water. In the background, a portable radio played her favorite station at a low volume.

Having combed her hair and gotten over her initial shock that Sebastian had actually come looking for her, she'd decided she would use this time to learn more about him. Her future, and the family she would create, required it of her. Because some day she'd have to tell her child about his or her father. What kind of man was he? Was he here to cajole her into marrying him to win that stupid competition?

Dare she let him into her life, allow him to learn more about her? It would be a cruelty if she ultimately decided against allowing him to participate in her child's life.

But that decision had not yet been made. And it was a big decision. One that needed all the supporting data she could acquire. Because no matter what, they would always be linked through their child. And that was an immense future to consider. Her wanting heart gushed and pleaded for her to invite him in and make him her own, while her logical brain put up a fit and insisted she ignore emotion and strive for practicality.

Stupid brain.

"It's peaceful out here," he commented as he set his plate aside. "Reminds me of summers at my grandparents' house south of Paris."

Pulled from the argument of brain versus heart, Azalea set her plate aside and rested her elbows on her knees, tilting her head to take him in. "Did they have a country place?"

"I suppose you would call it a château, but it was small and on many acres. Grandmother was the barefoot gardening sort who always greeted me with a spin."

"A spin?"

"She loved to dance anywhere, any time. She's the one who gave me a love for dancing."

"I don't think I've ever had more fun dancing than that night with you." Nor had she been more attracted, and downright sexually invigorated by his refreshing demeanor. Not what she'd expected from a man who knew how to wear an expensive suit. "Not many men care to loosen up like that. Especially one in such a fancy suit."

He brushed a trouser leg. He'd abandoned the suit coat, undone a few buttons at his collar and rolled up his white sleeves. Azalea decided it was his idea of comfort. "I'm all about suits, Zee."

"I suppose, since it's the family business. But with a little dancing included now and then?"

"Absolutely. I looked forward to those summers my mom would deposit me at the château to stay for weeks while she gallivanted off with her latest lover. My grandparents had a mangy dog and some chickens. And an insufferable goat."

"Goats are like that."

"They are. I even used to run barefoot in the grass." He eyed her bare feet. "So I'm not a complete slicker."

"You do earn points for that. But when was the last time your feet touched grass? I'm betting it hasn't been since those childhood summers."

"Is that a challenge?" He leaned in, tipping his glass against hers. "Because I'm all about challenges."

Yes, like finding a wife to give birth to his heir? Dare she spend the next day with him *without* telling him she carried his baby?

Oh, brain, just concede to heart!

"What's going on in there?" He tapped her temple and shifted to sit closer to her. "You're too serious for the fun-loving Zee I remember."

"You hardly know me."

"That's why I'm here. To learn more."

"Hmm, well, I do have moments that do not involve dancing wildly and tossing down champagne and tiny snacks."

"Oh, yes?" He paused, tilting his head to listen, and she noticed the sprightly song on the radio. "You know this one?"

At her affirmative nod, he stood and tugged her to stand on the porch. He spun her once under his arm, and they swirled into a few steps.

"Did your grandmother teach you this?" she called between bounces. She didn't know the dance exactly, but Petunia Grace had once been a competitive dancer during Azalea's preteen years.

"Of course! Grandmama loved the American dances."

With that he lifted her and twirled her around. Azalea thrust out her arms, her hair spilling out and a laugh gushing up. And when they whirled to a stop and he carefully set her down, he slid a hand along her cheek and studied her eyes with his beautiful, soulful, gray-blue eyes. From the frenzy of the dance to the sudden overwhelming *connection* of his gaze. She swallowed. Her heart resumed its swell in response. Tilting onto her toes, she kissed him.

A familiar place, this kiss. She didn't feel tentative or wary. Sebastian's heat coaxed her deeper and she reveled in the easy clash of tastes, textures and a hint of cherry sparkling water topping it off. As she leaned against his chest, her hands glided up and along his shoulders. Broad and straight. Her mighty rescuer in tailored armor. Her Parisian hero.

Breaking the kiss, she tilted her head against his shoulder and they swayed to the slower song that whispered behind them. The moment felt perfect, like something she needed to preserve in memory. So years from now she could tell the tale to her child.

"I'm glad you found me," she said without thinking her words through. It had been a confession. A true one. Her heart always spoke before her brain. "I missed you."

"I'm here now."

Yes, now. For less than twenty-four hours that she must wrap her arms around and squeeze out every moment. To remember forever. To tell stories about the man who danced her so silly they immediately followed it up with making a baby. Never would she have planned such a situation. However, this was not one of Azalea

Grace's bad choices. And there was not a thing about it she would change.

If only she could blurt it out…*tell him*. But something kept her tongue in place. A worry that she might lose what little hold she yet had on him. Or more so, that he may want her for something she wasn't willing to agree to.

Behind them Stella mooed. The cow didn't need to be fed. And Azalea had no intention of listening to a cow's insistence she tell the man *right now*.

"Do you have a guest room?" he asked on a whisper.

Her dad called her old bedroom the guest room now. A hint that she should be moving along?

"It's my room."

His brow quirked. "I wasn't going to ask to sleep separate from you tonight. And it seems that we are both guests in this home. Shall we?" He hooked an arm and she glanced down at the plates and goblets. "We'll clean that up in the morning. Right now, I need to kiss your skin. Everywhere."

A quiet hush gasped from her very being. "Yes."

Hours later, both of them lying naked on the bed, with the sheets off and the open window beckoning inside a sultry breeze, Azalea turned toward Sebastian. It was dark in the room because there was no moon. One of the things about living in the country? No ambient city lights. She loved it. Though she would like to see his eyes right now.

Stroking her finger along his face, she followed the jut of his jawline back to his head and up to his earlobe.

"What are you doing?" he asked quietly.

"Memorizing you. You've got a sharp jawline. I like it." She trailed her fingers down his neck and along his shoulder to a bicep. "I'm guessing you do more than dance at perfume parties to get these muscles. Gym?"

"There's a weight room in my building. But I do run when I can."

"So, you could chase me across a field?"

"I'll certainly give it a go if the opportunity presents itself." He leaned in and kissed the base of her neck. His soft hair tickled her chin. "It's nice out here. So peaceful. Where will you go when your dad sells this place?"

"Not sure yet. I enjoy wide-open spaces. But I like the connection that London offers and sometimes all this rural charm really does annoy a girl. I mean, it takes some effort to pick up a few snacks."

"Sounds like you're stuck between the convenience of a big city and the peace of a smaller town."

"I suppose I am."

"What about Paris? It's a big city, but there is something less busy about it than London."

"Are you suggesting I move to Paris?"

"I wouldn't mind you living in my city. I'd get to see you more often."

"Sebastian..." She dropped her hand to the sheet. "What are you doing? This thing between us, you know it's only a..."

A fling? What *was* it? Because it felt big. Like something she could welcome into her life. Something she *should* welcome into her life. Into her burgeoning family. And yet... It could only ever be a dream. And wouldn't it be best to simply leave it as a dream?

"I don't want it to be a fling, Zee."

Neither did she. But she also knew what she didn't want. "I don't want to do a long-distance relationship."

"You could move to the French countryside?"

"Sebastian."

"What? I'm tossing out ideas."

"We've known each other for less than forty-eight hours. And yes, what we have when we're together is good. Really good."

"Feels soul-deep," he said. "I mean, I can just

be with you, sitting on a porch, and that feels right."

Darn him for picking up on that intense connection. But thinking in such terms would only distract her from her staunch need to not settle for something that could never be real. Her mother had left her dad because she'd felt confined, stifled. How could Azalea possibly feel free under the thumb of a millionaire who wanted her for reasons that had nothing to do with love?

And yet, her fantasies of marriage and family had been recently renewed, treading right alongside the desire for a man who seemed too good to be true.

"Just because we're getting along well doesn't mean it will always be good," she said. "Besides, how will my living closer to you work when you have a wife and child?"

He rolled to his back and sighed. "I don't know."

That he didn't protest such a scenario meant it wasn't something he wanted to budge on. He had to find a wife. And have a child.

"I haven't seriously thought about that competition in weeks," he offered in the darkness. "I've been too focused on my dad's recovery and...you. Despite my busy schedule, I had to get away to find you. And now that I have, I question how to move forward. I want us to be a couple, Zee. But it feels as though you don't want it—"

"I do," she rushed out. A foolish outburst?

Oh, heart!

If she told him the real reason she wanted him, it would be as forced as his needing to find a wife. She wanted to be with Sebastian because she was falling in love with him, not because she felt beholden to him. Or because she was having his child and needed an official paper to give the baby legitimacy.

You want to make a real family. Mother. Baby. And father. You know you do.

He kissed the top of her head and slid a hand down to cup her derriere. "Let's sleep on it. Tomorrow is a new day. And I get to spend it with you."

He didn't say anything else. He didn't need to. She felt the same. Getting to spend time with him was a treat.

He would leave tomorrow, though. The idea of telling him she was pregnant suddenly felt manipulative. Like a means to keep him in her life. It wasn't like that. She'd thought about it. Debated the pros and cons with Stella. She was prepared to do the mother thing on her own. With the support of her family. She'd told Dahlia about it and her sister had offered to help her find a place to live and a job and day care. She hadn't told her dad yet. She would when he returned from vacation.

Now, to tell the man who needed a wife and child in order to secure his future that he'd already succeeded in meeting half that stipulation? Or to just step back and allow him to leave and have his own life in a world that she felt wasn't quite the right fit for her?

CHAPTER SEVEN

A DREAM-OBLITERATING SOUND woke Sebastian. He bolted upright in bed and muttered, "What the..."

It sounded again, long, obnoxious and...crowing. His entire musculature twinged tightly.

He swore.

The gentle touch of a hand to his back soothed reassuringly. He remembered where he was. On a farm. *Of all places.* But he was with her. And that made the next crow—still annoying.

"It's just Big Bruce," Zee whispered. "He's waking up the flowers. Lay down. It's early."

No kidding, it was early. Waking up the flowers? He didn't understand that. What did a cockerel have to do with—? Another crow crept into his spine and froze there.

The room was dark. He...couldn't exactly form thoughts beyond that. But the hand stroking his back chased away the chill and lured him to snuggle against the delicious warmth of Azalea. His Zee.

No obnoxious, crowing fowl could spoil that wondrousness.

Azalea rolled over in bed to find Sebastian smiling at her in the soft morning light.

"That cockerel is not my favorite part of this visit," he said quietly.

"Big Bruce is a noisy fellow."

"Agreed. Let's stay in bed all day and do what we did last night six more times."

"Six? You're awfully motivated."

"Too much? I'll settle for five."

She leaned in and kissed his nose and snugged her entire body against the length of his. Mmm, he was firm in all the right places. "Five, it is. But."

"But?"

At that moment, Big Bruce crowed.

"That," she said. "If I don't head out to feed the wildlife there will be a revolt."

"The life of a farmer?"

"I prefer rural princess, actually."

"Has a nice ring to it. Can I distract you for five minutes before you rush off to tend the animals?" He nudged the firmest part of him against her thigh.

"Absolutely."

* * *

After Zee left the bed, Sebastian showered and dressed. They'd only had time for two orgasms before she'd fled to tend the crowing and mooing menagerie. He'd claim the other three, or four, later.

The room was small but the bed had served as a cozy love nest. The entire place was minuscule compared to what he was accustomed to. But for the lack of maids who left his towels out and organized his fridge ingredients by color, he found he didn't mind the tiny home. Everything was an arm's reach away. He'd not had to walk across a vast closet to find anything.

The cockerel's crow tightened his muscles.

"Big Bruce and I will have words today," he muttered.

As for him and Zee, they had come together as if they'd never been apart. Sure, she'd been initially awkward, but a dance and some kisses had reminded them both that what they had was magical.

"There you go again," he muttered as he wandered down the hallway, "thinking like a romantic."

He hadn't a romantic bone in his body. Truly. Hell, Sebastian Mercier didn't know a thing about romance and love. He'd not witnessed as much growing up. No heart-fluttering, gushing examples had filled his learning brain. Affection had been so fleeting he felt quite sure he was incapable of loving another person.

And yet, the fact he stood here in this tiny cottage, had been woken at dawn by an annoying bird, and now sought to spend the day with a sweet rural princess must allude to some part of his heart softening to the idea of love and romance.

Or was it that he simply needed a wife? A means to an end. And Zee offered an option.

When he thought of it that way, his skin prickled. It sounded so clinical. And certainly, Zee was not the sort of woman who would ever agree to become a convenient bride. Yet he could never give her the love and romance she deserved if he hadn't a clue how those emotions worked.

He'd thought to come here to see if they still had a connection. If not, he'd have headed home to pursue the next candidate for wife. Yet their reunion had been anything but cold and distant. The passion they shared filled him in ways that surprised him. Could he possibly convince Zee to marry him?

Down in the small room before the back door he studied a neat shelving unit that housed shoes, boots and various caps, hats and gloves. Ah, here was a tidy setup. The rubber boots on the bottom looked about his size. And they fit.

"When in Rome," he muttered. Make that *when on a farm*.

He gave a stomp to each boot. Not much for comfort, but they would serve a purpose. The mud-green color clashed terribly with his gray, checked trousers, but he'd not packed comfort clothing, so this look would have to do.

"They could be more stylish with a buckle and perhaps a leather pull tab," he decided.

L'Homme Mercier did not offer shoes in their line. Something to consider? If they ever went with a rustic line, for sure.

Stepping outside, he wandered across the tidy porch and stepped down onto a neat stone walk. The outdoor shower deserved a nod of approval. A few decorative pots of frothy grass rose almost as high as his head and gave off a lemon scent. The path veered in a curving fashion toward the blue barn. With the sun high in the pale sky he wished he'd worn a T-shirt or something lighter than his white button-up, but a roll of each sleeve provided some relief from the humid heat.

He could do rustic as well as anyone. Who would have thought? Certainly, though, his family would scoff to see him now. If it wasn't luxury, artisan-made, an original, or reeking of old money, it wasn't worth the notice. Cows and cockerels? The indignity!

His family didn't have to know about this trip to Ambleside. Nor did they have to know about Azalea. She was…

What was she, exactly? She had stuck in his brain for so long that he'd had to find her. And now that he had, he wanted to stay and never leave her side. Find a way to keep her in his life. Though he much preferred they be together in a less rural setting, he could manage for the duration of this visit. Which would be too short.

If he got involved with Zee, then what would become of his quest to find a wife? He couldn't have a lover and a fake wife. Or? Well? No. It just wouldn't do. He was not a French king or even the president of the country. Despite the press's tendency to label them careless, pleasure-seeking playboys, even the Merciers had their standards.

Might Zee consider becoming his wife? A name on an official piece of paper, who wasn't required to love him or receive love in return. But certainly, it did demand she give him an heir.

Sebastian scrubbed his fingers across the back of his head. He could never fake it with Zee. And not faking it would only complicate it all and confuse his emotions.

Then again, he was no man to back down from a challenge. Especially one that offered such a delicious prize as the freckle-faced rural princess. And the clock was ticking.

"Play it by ear," he muttered as he wandered toward the open barn door. "It's only been a day."

Yes, and things could change. His heart might simply be in the throes of a new and unique interest and passion. Everything cooled. That was a given. As his father had so often said to his sons, "The glow rubs off quickly. And then you're left with disinterest and the itch for something new."

Easy enough for Roman Mercier to say when he hadn't been presented with a win-it-or-lose-the-company ultimatum. There was nothing Sebastian wanted more than to claim the CEO position of L'Homme Mercier.

Not even Azalea Grace? his inner devil whispered.

Well. Which did he want more? Could he really claim attachment to a woman he knew so little? The CEO position meant more. It did.

"Zee?" he called as he entered the cool shade of the barn.

No reply. He wandered through and spied the blonde combing a rather monstrous cow with a long brown coat that flowed over its eyes and horns.

Sebastian had never been around large farm animals. He was rarely around dogs or cats, though he did favor a mellow, napping cat over the oft-rambunctious dog. Those stays at his grandparents' had only ever introduced him to one old dog who could barely wander from his bed to the feeding bowl. There had been the occasional turtles and snakes. Creatures that had fascinated his younger self. And heaven forbid he ever encounter another goat.

Slowing his pace, he cautiously approached, noting there was a smaller cow at the end of a fenced area, nipping at foliage that grew wild against a fence post.

"Why do you call me Zee?" she asked, keeping her attention on the midsection of the beast that she combed.

"You don't like it?" He winced at the scent of manure that rose from all around him. Yet it was topped with a sweet grassy note. He much preferred a perfume-doused room.

"I don't mind. Most friends call me Lea."

"Well, I'm not a friend." But what was he exactly? "Is this beast what you would call a bull?"

She smirked at him as he stopped a good five feet from the animal. He glanced back to the barn. Sprinting distance, if necessity required.

"Stella is a girl. Not a bull."

"*This* is Stella? I thought she was your best friend?"

"She is."

"I see." And here he'd thought her best friend would be a human. Well, he should have guessed, eh? "But she has horns."

"Girl cows can have horns. Specific breeds, that is."

"I didn't know that. She's..." He bent to find the creature's eyes but the long coat covered them completely. "How can she see?"

"Her coat moves when she walks. She knows where you are. She smells you."

"As I smell her." The beast snorted and bobbed her head. Sebastian took a precautionary step back. "Sorry," he provided. "I'm sure you smell lovely to other cows."

"I see you found my dad's wellies," Zee said.

"Do you think he'll mind?"

"Not at all. It's messy out here. Come closer. Give my girl a pat on the nose. She likes affection."

"Very well." Not about to appear afraid of an animal she was obviously comfortable to stand beside, he carefully approached, stretching out an arm until he was just near enough to gently pat her nose. It was...warm and had a soft leathery texture. The beast nudged against his palm. So he stepped closer and gave her nose a gentle rub. "She likes that."

"Stella is a flirt. She'll have you wrapped around her horns in no time."

"I'm not sure I like the idea of such a scenario."

"I didn't mean it like that. Like having you wrapped around her little finger. You know. Maybe you don't. It might have gotten lost in translation."

"Indeed." And yet, he was perfectly content should Zee wish to keep him wrapped about her pinkie finger.

The smaller cow now wandered over, its nostrils flaring as it scented him. Sebastian stepped closer to Azalea.

"She's only five months old," she said. "I think she's going to take after her mom. Goes for the handsome men, she does."

Patting the little one's nose, he was happy to note that it stopped the beast from getting closer to him. "Do you have a lot of handsome men visiting your animals?"

She chuckled. "Nope. Well, my dad is handsome. And he babies them like they were his children. I think that's good, Stella. You look gorgeous." Zee wrapped her arms about the cow's head for a hearty hug.

"You don't worry about those horns?"

"I'm careful. So." She tucked the comb in a pocket of her overalls. "I'd offer you breakfast but I haven't had time to do grocery shopping.

How about we head into the village for a hearty British brekkie?"

"If that means protein and eggs, I'm in."

"Great. You like to ride a bike?"

Sebastian strode after her as she headed through the barn, hanging up the comb as she did. "Bike? Are you serious?"

"Would you prefer we jog?" She chuckled but didn't reassure him that she was indeed joking with him.

And Sebastian swallowed to think that this trip to find the woman of his dreams might just challenge him in ways he never could have imagined.

They did not bike into the village. Azalea had been teasing. The look of utter horror on Sebastian's face when she'd suggested they might pedal in was probably the exact look she hadn't been able to see when Big Bruce had woken him before the crack of dawn.

Poor guy. Farm life could be tough for the uninitiated. But hadn't he said he was a runner? Probably he required fancy running togs and a dedicated path through a city park for such a venture.

Parking her dad's old car on a side street, she then led Sebastian down the quaint cobbled street to her favorite breakfast café.

* * *

After a huge breakfast of bacon, eggs, beans and toast, and a rosemary-seasoned blend of summer vegetables, she led Sebastian on a walk along the river that was hugged on one side by tight hedgerows. He snapped a few selfies of them standing before the Bridge House, then she tugged him down a pathway. The hiking trail was well worn, so the fact that he wore designer shoes without rubber treads wouldn't be a problem.

"It's beautiful out here," he commented as they paused on a hillock to look over Lake Windermere.

A corvid flew over their heads, frighteningly low.

"They're looking for food scraps," Azalea explained. "From the tourists. They come here for the hiking and scenery. It is a lovely place."

"A place you plan to stay in forever?"

He really wanted to nail down her future plans. He'd asked much the same last night in bed.

She leaned against a wood fence post and studied his profile. If she checked the entry for handsome in the dictionary, she felt sure to find Sebastian's picture there. With an addendum warning all women to proceed with caution.

"I fled London to lick my wounds after I

broke up with Lloyd. I have a tendency to make bad life choices when it comes to men."

He flicked a concerned look her way.

She shrugged. "I'm not sure where I'll go after Dad returns from Australia. I don't want to intrude on his new relationship. He and Diane are quite smart together. She makes him smile again. And that's a good thing. Besides, he plans to sell, so I need to pack up and find my own place in this world."

And if they continued on this course of conversation, she'd have to tell him everything. That information was not something she wanted to reveal with tourists wandering by.

"Tell me about your parents," she said. "Are they the sort who would welcome you to stay after a breakup?"

"Perhaps my mother would if she was staying in Paris at the time. My parents are… My father has never married any of his children's mothers."

"Oh. So you and your brother…?"

"Philippe has a different mother than mine. It's why we are only six months apart in age. And I just got a new set of twin brothers nine months ago. Another girlfriend for my dad. Good ole Dad is still single."

"I think they are called playboys. Or baby daddies."

Sebastian laughed and clasped her hand. "That is most definitely Roman Mercier. The man is set in his ways."

"And those ways involve pitting his sons against one another and forcing them to marry? I can dismiss his roguish ways, but really, Sebastian, a man who has never married is asking his sons to do so? I find that hypocritical."

"I try not to consider it too much. And since the strokes, I've noticed more urgency to his manner. He's tasted mortality. He wants to ensure L'Homme Mercier is in good hands before he leaves this world."

"I don't see why both sons can't work together."

"If you knew about the changes and direction Philippe wants to take the company you would understand. He wants to add a women's division."

"And you don't?"

"What part of L'Homme Mercier says women's clothing?"

"Nothing wrong with expanding, is there? The women's market must be much bigger than the men's."

He shook his head and scoffed. "We are a menswear company. Always have been. And should remain so. I'm not against taking the brand to new levels, keeping up with the trends, but there's no need to cater to the female clientele. So many other designers do it and do it well."

"I understand that." She tilted onto her toes to kiss him. A means to assuage what she guessed was a touchy subject that might have just raised his blood pressure a few digits. "I hope you win."

"You're just saying that because you like me."

"I do like you. You're smart. You're handsome. And you like to dance. We have fun together. But."

The fact that he'd tracked her down meant that he hadn't advanced his plans to find a wife. Or had he? Oh, bother.

"But?" He clasped her hand and pressed the back of it against his lips. Thinking something through? "Am I one of your bad choices, Zee?"

Damn. She shouldn't have put that one out there.

"Not completely. But well, what *is* this, Sebastian? You've already told me you wouldn't consider me marriage material."

"And you've told me you'd never marry me."

"I would not. I don't want to be a pawn in your family competition."

"I get that but… Zee, I like you. Very much. And that *like* puts a wrench in the competition."

"How so?"

"I'd much rather spend time with you than

seek a potential wife. A woman I fully intend to marry only on paper. Show my father the male heir. Deed done."

"Sebastian, how can you say that? Much as I care about you, it offends me that you'd treat a woman like that. And use a child in such a manner."

"I don't know how else to do this, Zee. Unless the perfect woman falls into my arms, I will be forced to find a facsimile wife to win the company. And I must win because L'Homme Mercier must remain as it is."

He couldn't know how hearing that devastated her. Azalea bowed her head. She could understand his desire to keep the family business as he wished it to remain. That his father had set such a ridiculous requirement was cruel to both his sons and to the woman trapped in a loveless marriage, and the resultant baby.

And that made her even more reluctant to reveal her news to him. He didn't need to know. Well, he did. But he didn't need to be a part of her life. Nor she his. That was optional. A choice she mustn't allow to be wrong.

How could she possibly tell him she was pregnant?

"Let's walk back to town and try out the bowling green I saw in the little green square near a pub," he suggested. "I haven't played the game since I was a kid."

"Sure." She clasped his hand and he led them back to the trail. "You're a bit of a kid yourself," she decided. "You like to have fun. That'll be a good thing when you're a dad."

"You think?" He squeezed her hand. "I do enjoy when I see my little brothers. They're adorable. I will strive to be a much different father to my children than my father is to me and my stepbrothers."

That was hopeful to hear. But the idea of raising a child in the Mercier family of men who did not feel love was necessary to commit did not appeal to Azalea at all.

CHAPTER EIGHT

SEBASTIAN WAS SURPRISED at how the red-feathered hen had settled comfortably against his stomach as he held it. Trusting. Zee had shown him how to carefully pick it up, protecting its wings and cupping its feet. Now he stroked its head softly and whispered in French that she was pretty.

Zee sat beside him with another hen in hand. She winked at him. Her wavy hair spilled across her cheek, and if he had not had his hands full, he would have brushed it aside.

How to convince her that marrying him would make them both happy? Did he believe that they could be happy together? It felt as though happiness were a possibility. And really, if he had to marry, why not to a woman with whom he genuinely enjoyed spending time?

"You're a natural," she said. "Ginger is in love with you."

"Ginger, eh?"

"Yep. And this is Posh." She tousled the elaborate feathers that spouted bodaciously from the top of her chicken's head as if a cheerleader's pom-pom. "That's Scary over there with the missing tail feathers. And… Sporty is over there chasing Daisy. She's the most athletic of the crew."

"Where's Baby?"

Zee sucked in her lower lip and cast him a worried glance. "Dad and Diane made coq au vin before they left for Australia."

"Oh." At that horrifying statement Sebastian could but hug his content fowl closer. Might he ever enjoy a chicken meal again after bonding with the sweet and snuggly Ginger?

"I know," she said. "But despite her name, Baby was getting long in her years. She wasn't laying anymore. She lived a good life."

"And you think *I'm* callous about this whole marriage thing."

"I would hardly compare eating a pet hen to faking a marriage."

"It's not—"

He wanted her to be wrong but she was closer to the truth than he was. How else *could* he manage such a situation? He wouldn't know love if it smacked him in the face. And that was what it was wont to do if it did occur and he had the audacity to insist on marriage.

"Let's not talk about that right now," he said.

"I'm enjoying this moment with you. I like that we can sit together and be quiet."

She laid her head on his shoulder. "And hug chickens."

"It's a nice break from my usual hectic schedule. And the sunset is unreal."

Pink, violet and brilliant streaks of gold painted the sky. He'd not taken a moment to notice the sunsets in Paris. It was a vibrant masterpiece. Just like Zee. And Ginger. The colors made him think of the first time he'd been introduced to embroidery work by one of the tailors. It wasn't utilized in suit-making but had been a hobby. The old man had crooked a finger, urging a young Sebastian to follow him into the back room at L'Homme Mercier. With a gleeful flash of his eyes, he'd then opened a sewing box to reveal a rainbow of embroidery threads and shown him the various needles. Sebastian had run his fingers over the silken threads, in awe. Perhaps that had been what had cemented his true interest in the creation of fine clothing, from the very basic stitches to the elegant fabrics and quality craftsmanship. It beat out machine-made factory clothing by everything.

He hadn't worked hands-on creating a suit in years. But there were days he wished the old tailor with the sparkle in his eyes was still around.

Sebastian would like to explore his collection of colored threads and create something.

As CEO of L'Homme Mercier he would take on more responsibility, yet at the same time he might be able to delegate to others some of his current duties that were tedious. It was his life. He honored hard work and talent, but he also appreciated this trip that allowed him to relax and not think about shipping schedules or clients or vendor complications.

"I don't want to go home," he blurted.

"I was wondering when you were going to leave. You said you would stay twenty-four hours. That's right about now."

"Do I have to leave?" he asked himself. Then he looked to Zee. "Do you want me to leave?"

"I want you to stay as long as you like."

"Then I'll stay. Because leaving you doesn't feel right. Don't you agree, Ginger?"

The chicken cooed quietly. Content. As he felt. Sitting beside Zee felt right.

"You don't have work to get back to?"

"I can manage another day," he decided. Maybe two? "I have a meeting on Friday with a supplier that I mustn't miss. He's traveling from Dubai."

"That gives us two more days."

"My stay won't be unwanted?"

"Honestly? I wish you could stay all summer." She kissed him and in the process her chicken squawked and made a fuss so she set it free. "How about I go in and make us something to eat."

"I'm quite hungry after our adventurous day."

"Great. I'll make chicken!" She got up, leaving Posh on the ground by his feet, looking up at him with a worried fowl stare.

"I'll protect you," he said to the hen. He scanned his gaze around the yard, sighting the other two birds. Stella wandered near the fence. "Should have done a head count on the poultry earlier."

On the other hand, if Big Bruce were sacrificed, he would not argue the quiet.

The next afternoon they hiked out across the hillocks and stones of the countryside along the bank of Lake Windermere.

Azalea chose a spot next to a low stone wall and laid out a plaid blanket near a crop of wild poppies, while Sebastian snapped some shots of the glassy blue lake and the lush greenery hugging it. It truly was as gorgeous as the tourist advertisements made it look. And it smelled like the real world, so verdant and full. And as luck would have it, she'd led them onto an unmarked trail that only the residents knew about, so unless some tourists got curious, they'd have this cozy little patch to themselves.

She'd packed a simple lunch of sandwiches,

fresh fruit, cheese and bottled water. Diane had made cream cheese cookies before leaving on holiday and had left them in the freezer. Azalea had been judiciously thawing but one a day as a treat. Today, she'd packed four.

Taking the stone path carefully, Sebastian returned to sit on the blanket beside her. "You say people come here to hike the mountains?"

"Yes, it's a big tourist draw. I mean, I don't know if the summits qualify as mountains but they give good exercise."

"Have you hiked them?"

"Yes, all around the area which is the National Forest. I can start out in the morning and not be seen until after sunset. There are sweet surprises all over, like tiny stone bridges, or enchanting tree-covered paths, and the Stagshaw Gardens. There's a waterfall that way in the Stock Ghyll woods. It's a lovely way to while away an afternoon. Oh, and there's the champion trees. It's a pretty walk among hundreds of different types of trees. My favorite is the sequoia."

"You're a real nature girl. I understand now why a big city does not appeal to you."

"And yet, a big-city man does offer appeal." She handed him a bottle of water, and he took her wrist and pulled her closer to kiss her.

Feeling like a heroine from a nineteenth century novel, Azalea decided the flutter in her chest and the warmth enveloping her neck was a genuine swoon. The man could own her with his slow and deep kisses. And that was a dangerous realization.

He bowed his forehead to hers and tapped her lips. "I'm glad your heart is not determined to find a rural lover wielding a pitchfork and wearing wellies."

Recalibrating her malfunctioning common sense, she sat up straight and lifted her chin. "Nothing wrong with that type. They are dependable, hardworking..." And yet...the one she had briefly dated had wanted her barefoot, pregnant and subservient. "Though I feel sure my princess inclinations would not be weathered well by such a hardy rural man. I do like to dress up and do the city life once in a while."

"You balance between the wilds and the urban," Sebastian said. "Princess one day, cow whisperer the next?"

"Works for me. But what about you? I don't fit in with your lifestyle, do I? I mean, Lloyd said it best when he—"

Another kiss made her realize that she had been about to spout nonsense and silliness. Lloyd was her past. The comments he had made about their differences were just his perspective. Common sense wasn't always fun, nor should it ruin a perfectly lovely picnic.

Sebastian said, "We are different, Zee. My grandmother used to read me a story when I was little. Something about a country mouse and a city mouse?"

"I think that story was more about one's ambitions and desires. Each has their own comfort zone. Of course, I believe it was the city mouse who lived in fear of the cat all the time. The country mouse was quite content to return home after a brief adventure in the big city."

"You think my ambitions are too much?"

"If they involve marrying a woman merely on paper to achieve a position?" She busied herself with unwrapping the sandwiches and cookies. It had just come out. It was the truth, to her. Even Sebastian had said as much.

"You think I should concede to Philippe in order to avoid a moral misstep?"

Who was she to tell him what he had the right to do or how to live his life? She couldn't even come to terms with how to proceed with her own life!

She handed him a sandwich and shook her head. "I think you should be true to your heart." And her heart performed a double beat in response to that statement.

Listen to me, it seemed to beg. *Are you being true to your heart?*

He nodded, taking a few bites. "I'm not even sure what my heart's truth is right now."

"My heart has a tendency to think before my brain does. It can sometimes be annoying. And I regret the things I do. But later, it always seems as though it was right."

"Even when it was a bad choice?"

"Even so." He wouldn't let that one drop. Sebastian Mercier was not a bad choice. Well, not as bad as some of her choices had been. "My heart speaks my truth. I just have to learn to listen to it and stop arguing for something different."

"What arguments have you with your heart right now?"

If he only knew. The one where she wanted to wrap him in her arms and never let him go. Tell him she was pregnant as a means to keep him in her life. Win the man she adored.

Stupid heart.

In this particular situation, her brain knew better. Nothing good could come of such a relationship because her heart could never really know if Sebastian's feelings for her were true or just manufactured to obtain the CEO position.

"Wow." He brushed breadcrumbs from his pant leg. "There really is an argument going on in there." He pointed to her chest, there where her heart pounded to be heard, to be acknowledged, to simply be followed. "Is it about me?"

She smirked and leaned back on her palms, stretching out her legs. "You know it is."

"I am honored to have found a position in your heart. Though it saddens me that it causes you internal struggle."

"Sebastian, you are a charmer. But we both know this can't go anywhere. So why not just enjoy what we have right now?"

"Then walk away from one another and proceed as if it didn't even happen?"

"Oh, I'll never forget you."

"Nor I you." He took her hand and pressed it over his heart. "My heart developed this weird little hole the morning I woke up and found you had snuck out, never to be seen again. And since then, it's been wanting to fit you into that hole. Someway, somehow."

Such a confession kicked her own heart, trying to convince it to comply. To be honest with her needs for her future. But her brain held her back. So much to consider now with the way her life had begun to unfold.

Shrugging, she offered him a treat. "How about a cookie to fill that hole?"

With a smirk, he took one and bit into it, turning to look across the lake. And Azalea knew that with or without him in her life, he would always be a part of her world.

She couldn't decide whether that was good,

bad or ugly. But mostly, she just wanted her heart to get its act together and win.

They walked back through Ambleside just as a city parade was coming to an end. The streets were packed with tourists and residents and so many children.

Sebastian noted they carried wood frames covered with flowers and long weedy leaves. "What did we miss?"

"It's the annual rush-bearing festival. Celebrates the cleaning out of the rushes from the churches. I guess it's become so commonplace to me I didn't even think to ask if you wanted to watch. Those wood frames are rush bearers. And the leafy things are rushes. They used to place them on the floors in medieval times as rugs and to keep things cleaner. Seems to me they might have been more of a big mess."

"Interesting." He paused at the edge of the crowd, taking in a crew of bustling children dashing about with rushes and flowers in hand. One of them ran up to him and with big, beaming eyes offered him a white flower.

Sebastian bent and took the flower. "Thank you."

The little girl, no more than five or six, winked at him, then performed a twirl and spun back into the procession alongside her friends. He stood and sniffed the blossom.

"You are a lady killer," Zee muttered. "But that was also the most adorable thing I've ever seen."

The look she flashed up at him landed in his heart like a warm beam of sunshine. It felt like admiration, perhaps even pride. And Sebastian had never felt more worthy of a woman's regard in his lifetime. Wow. It wasn't an overwhelming feeling, yet it seemed to flood his system with a knowing warmth, a quiet joy. The noise of the parade faded out and he smiled to himself, sinking deeply into the moment. It needed to be honored, recognized. And enjoyed.

Azalea Grace had a power over his heart that should frighten him, but instead he wanted to sway toward her and allow her open access to it. To him. To anything she desired that would see that look of pride beaming at him again.

"Sebastian?"

Surfacing from the feeling with a tilt of his head that allowed back in all the ambient noise of life, he gripped her hand and gave it a squeeze. Tucking the white flower into Zee's hair, he kissed her forehead.

"Back to the farm," she said, unaware of his incredible journey of emotion. "You've got a train to catch."

* * *

After witnessing Zee in her natural environment, Sebastian realized what he wanted was not something he could have. They were two different people. Living in two very different places. With two different focuses. And while millions of couples all around the world obviously made similar situations work, he sensed Zee's reluctant to give it a go. She pulled him to her while at the same time pushed him away. Such inadvertent machinations had the potential to drive him mad.

So he must be done with it.

All the proud, admiring glances in the world would never change their situation.

If she wasn't willing to give this thing they had a try, then he must set back his shoulders, chin up, and walk away from her. Much as he adored her, if she couldn't see a future between them, then he must stop trying to prod the dead horse, so to speak.

Thinking of animals, he thought of Zee, out in the barn tending Stella and Daisy.

He paused in folding the dress shirt he'd packed and peered out the window. He'd called for a car, which would arrive soon. And then he would leave. Never to see her again?

He stuffed his shirt and trousers into the suitcase, not caring if they wrinkled. Perhaps he had one last chance to woo her, to convince her that they could be more than just a brief fling. Should he take it? Would he wound her by further involving her in the mess of a future life he must create to win the prize?

"One more try," he muttered.

CHAPTER NINE

AZALEA PRESSED HER palms against the wood fence behind the barn. With a few deep inhales, the wooziness she'd felt passed. Morning sickness. It had occurred two or three times in the last month. And not necessarily in the morning. A quick online search had told her it could occur at any hour. She hadn't vomited yet. But the nauseous feeling rose so quickly all she could do was focus on her breathing until it subsided.

She could be thankful it hadn't attacked when in Sebastian's presence.

By her calculations she was three months pregnant. When she'd taken the test a month earlier, she'd surprised herself with her reaction. No tears. No regrets. She'd been excited to know a new life was growing inside her. While she'd not come to a decision regarding whether to tell Sebastian—that nasty competition spoiled everything—she did realize she was strong and independent. Women did the single mother thing all the time. She could manage.

"Really?" she scoffed. "How's that going to work without a job or home?"

Sure, she could stay here at Grace Farm. But her dad intended to put up the For Sale sign when he returned from Australia. And she was quite sure she couldn't tag along with him and Diane to their next location. If they even bought a permanent home. The twosome planned to travel for a while before settling down. Azalea would not be a third wheel, even if one of the other wheels was her dad. Especially so.

She needed to find a home and a job within the next few months or she would be left homeless and sporting a baby propped on her hip. Not the way she wanted to begin life as a mother.

She could ask Sebastian for help. But that would mean revealing all to him.

Sebastian had disconcerting views about family and children. The family he created in order to gain control of L'Homme Mercier would be fake. And the idea of even considering them as a couple, possibly married, didn't sink in right. She might never know if he were marrying her because she was the mother of his child or because he wanted to win a competition.

And even if love were involved, she would never force a man to marry her just to make things look right. The world had changed. Single mothers were no longer ostracized or sneered at. And forcing a man to be a father, simply to make a family, could go the wrong way and the child could suffer because of it.

Though she wouldn't mind a little financial assistance from him.

"What to do?" she asked Stella, who currently rocked her head against the fence for a good scratch. "I have to tell him. It's only fair. But I don't want him to feel coerced. Or to take advantage of the situation. How am I going to do this?"

He was leaving soon. An important meeting tomorrow morning required he return to Paris. She couldn't guess how he would react to her news. She didn't want it to turn into an argument or a sob-fest or, worse, an obligation.

She stroked the cow's side, giving her a firm pat. "What do you think, Stella? The next step I take is going to steer my life. I just want to make the right choice this time."

Rain seemed appropriate for his departure. It began fitful and heavy, then settled to drizzle. The air smelled like ozone and flowers. It really was a kick to notice that unadulterated scent.

According to the tracking on his app, the car he'd called for would arrive in about twenty minutes. His suitcase sat near the front door. The wellies he'd borrowed were cleaned and placed neatly in their cubby. And Zee... She'd been strangely aloof since they'd returned home following the rush-bearing festival. When he'd suggested they have sex one last time she'd said she needed to feed the cows.

Really?

He suspected she might be feeling the same way he did. Parting would tear out his heart. As much as he wanted to stay forever, though, it wasn't possible. She'd drawn a line. He must respect that. And remember that for one amazing moment he had earned that look of pride from her. A look he would never forget.

In the kitchen, the white flower blossom gifted him by the little girl sat in a small glass vase on the table. He heard the back door swing shut on its creaky hinges.

"Zee?"

"Right there! Just washing the mud off my legs."

When she wandered into the kitchen, she was barefoot, wearing a simple floral dress that was a little wet from the rain. Her hair hung in loose wet waves over her shoulders. A beautiful mess.

"You're ready to leave? I'm so sorry I lost track of time. When does the car arrive?"

"Soon." He set his coat on the suitcase and took her in his arms. He swayed, sliding a hand up her back. "One last dance?"

Hugging up against him she followed his slow

steps, her head against his shoulder. They didn't need music to find their rhythm; they'd been in sync since the moment they'd met. Every move, every glance, every shared smile felt meant to be. Fated? He'd never thought much about fate and destiny but it did feel special.

And yet, he noticed her careful separation from him, the sudden absence of her head from his shoulder, the misstep as she turned the opposite direction he'd intended.

Sebastian blurted, "You've been avoiding me since we returned to the cottage."

"I..." She exhaled and stepped from his embrace, nodding. "Sorry. This is difficult."

"I feel the same. But I thought you had decided this wasn't possible?"

"This?" She blew out a breath and rubbed a hand over her belly.

"Well, us, of course. Have you had a change of heart? Zee, I know this whole marriage thing isn't fair to you. But I need you to understand that you are set aside from that. That's an odd way to put it. You—I care about you, Zee. I think I could fall in love with you."

She tugged in her lower lip and winced.

"Please don't make that face. I'll take it personally." He held up his hand, pinkie extended.

She sighed but didn't return the pinkie hug. Oh, the unbearable weight of rejection.

"I'm sorry. It's just the love thing," she said. "You only think you're in love. Or could fall in love. You can't say, with certainty, you are in love. I know it's complicated. Oh, Sebastian. There's something I need to tell you. And I've been sitting on it since you arrived, unsure how to reveal it."

At that moment a car rolled up the drive and honked.

Sebastian took out his phone and texted the driver that he'd be five minutes. "What is it, Zee? When I say I think could fall in love, that's it exactly. I'm not sure I've ever been in love before. And God knows it's not a thing I've ever gotten much of in my life. This is a new feeling for me. Allow me some measure to figure that out?"

"You weren't in love with the woman who fled the back of the limo that night we met?"

"No. Amie and I had dated for only three weeks."

"Why did she run off?"

"Because for some reason she was offended by my proposal." He knew the reason. Amie was not stupid. Love was an important ingredient to marriage. Or so he suspected. She'd made the right choice. "She tossed the ring at me and left. I was honest with you about that situation. It's the past. Has no bearing on what's going on with us. Zee, we can make this work. Paris isn't that far away—"

"Sebastian, I'm pregnant."

"And I can— What?" The heartfelt argument sluiced from his brain like a flood. What she'd just said. Had he heard her correctly? "You just said..."

Zee splayed out her hands. "I took a test—two of them—and I'm pregnant. It happened that night in Paris. I haven't been with anyone else, so I know it's yours. Promise. And I know what this means in the competition sense of things to you. But it can't be like that. I won't allow it to be."

He took her by the upper arms. Big blue eyes peered up at him. No freckles caught in the crinkles though, because she wasn't smiling. Was that sadness in her irises? Why was she not bubbling over with joy? Did she not feel the same, sudden intensity of emotion that he did?

"Zee," he breathed. His heartbeats raced. Every muscle in his body wanted to follow that race. What a rush of emotion and— "Do you tell me true?"

She nodded.

"But that's..."

What was that? He was going to be a father? That sealed that part of the competition—but no. He mustn't react that way. It was... Not right. Unfair to Zee. Unfair to his own feelings.

What *were* his feelings about this unexpected

announcement? Besides the fact that he felt as if something inside him were actually bubbling. Was it joy? It felt akin to the feeling he'd savored while they'd stood watching the parade.

"Really?" A smile wiggled on his lips and he didn't fight it. This news felt…not wrong. Though he wasn't sure if it was quite right, either. At least, not to judge from her lack of enthusiasm. "Zee, I wish you had told me about this sooner. We could have talked about it."

He'd given up on asking her to marry him after seeing her thriving in her natural habitat, but with this news…might he have asked her after all?

"There's nothing to discuss. I've decided that I don't want to involve myself, and this baby, in the Mercier family drama. I just thought it was only fair to tell you about it. You are the father. You have a right to know. I'll be fine on my own. I'm not going to ask anything of you."

"But you must. Ask me for everything! Zee, this is *my* baby."

The car honked.

Sebastian cursed. He stuck his head out the doorway and gestured for the driver to be patient. "I can't believe this. I need to process this. We must discuss what this means. Zee?"

"I know. I apologize for saving this for the last minute. I think this is as cruel as I've ever been to a person. And I'm not proud of that. But I was scared of your reaction. That you might want to use me and the baby to win the game you're playing with your brother. Even though I do desire family and…finding someone who cares about me."

"But—"

She thrust up a palm to stop his desperate plea. "Just accept that I have to do it this way."

He nodded, though it wasn't a means to agreement. It was merely a reaction to—such a surprise. Processing it would take some thought. Never would he have expected her to reveal such a thing as… "I'm going to be a father?"

She shrugged. "Well, it's your sperm. I'll be doing all the mothering and childcare."

He didn't like that she put it that way. It relegated him to the side, to not being a part of the baby's life. Did he want that? He needed a child. But that was a need created by his desire for career advancement. For the very thing he most wanted in life.

Another honk annoyed him, but he reacted to the rude prompt—and Zee's seeming indifference to his heart—by grabbing his suitcase. "We have not discussed this properly. You owe me that much. Promise me, when your father returns, you'll come to Paris so we can talk about this like adults. Zee?"

She nodded. "Of course. It's only fair."

She was so resigned. His heart broke. No joyous bubbles. Just utter ache. Was he not worthy of her recognizing him as the father of her child? Did she not want him in her life? And here he'd made plans to attempt to woo her one last time…

"At the very least don't you want to come to Paris to see me again?" It felt like a childish plea, but he was at odds, unsure about anything right now.

"I do, but… This is just so big, Sebastian. I need time—"

"I do, too. But I also need us to handle this. Together." He opened the door. "When will your dad return?"

"A few weeks."

"Then…here." He took out his phone and started a text. "I'm sending you my address… along with all the digital entry codes. As soon as you can, come to Paris. If I'm not home, you walk right in. My place is yours." A tap of his finger sent her the information. With reluctance, he lifted his head and nodded. "I'll see you in a few weeks?"

She nodded and managed a weak smile.

A kiss would be most appropriate, but something held him back from leaning in to claim that delicious connection. Things had changed between them. So suddenly. And he honestly didn't know whether to label it good or terrible.

No pinkie hugs this time. He'd lost that connection. Or rather, she had indicated it wasn't what she wanted.

Turning and taking the cobblestone pathway to the waiting car was the hardest move Sebastian had ever had to make. Raindrops spat at his skin. He put his suitcase in, slid into the back and closed the door, and the car rolled away. Away from a woman who dazzled him. A woman for whom his heart beat. A woman who allowed him to see the world in a new way, or rather, reminded him of a simpler time when he'd been a child and had enjoyed life.

A woman…who carried his child.

"Mon Dieu," he muttered as he rubbed a temple.

Was he doing the right thing? Walking away from her right now? The meeting could—well, it was important. But he could reschedule. The client was flying in from Dubai but he could put him up in a hotel for a day or two…

"No." Zee had asked for time to think about this. As well, he needed to think about it. A few weeks before her father returned?

This was going to be the longest fortnight of his life.

CHAPTER TEN

Oliver Grace and Diane had returned to the farm a week ago. After Diane left for town to pick up groceries, Azalea decided it time to tell her dad she was pregnant. He'd looked surprised but had immediately pulled her into a hug and kissed her forehead. Motherhood, or rather nurturing, had always been her true calling, he'd declared. Then he'd asked if the baby would call him Grandpa or maybe Pops?

That had been much easier than how she'd expected the talk to go. Even the information about Sebastian, and his family competition, had been listened to with a quiet nod from her dad.

"You've got to do what feels right in your heart," he said now as they sat out on the porch steps. "I'm here for you, Lea, you know that. And I agree that London isn't the place for you. But..." He sighed. "You can't hide here forever."

"You posting the For Sale sign out front yesterday was a very obvious clue."

"It's not even that, Lea. If you wanted to stay here and we could work out a means for rent, I'd be behind that."

Yet she knew he needed the sale of the land and house to finance his future. A future of new dreams and adventure that Diane had been detailing since they'd returned. Next stop? The United States, starting with New York City! Diane had already booked a room and purchased Broadway tickets for October in hopes the property sold quickly.

"But speaking as a man," he said as he clasped her hand, "Sebastian does deserve more than the quick five minutes you gave him before he had to leave."

The manner in which she'd told Sebastian, as the driver waited to whisk him away, had been cruel. She'd panicked, prolonging the reveal for far too long. He would have stayed if she'd asked it of him. But the moment had felt like ripping off a plaster. She'd just wanted to toss it aside and not look at it, so seeing him off had been all she could manage at the time.

"Go to him, Lea. Talk to him."

"I will. I just…"

"No more excuses. Stella will survive without you. In fact, I spoke to Burke the other day." The owner of the farm on the opposite side of the lake from Grace Farm. "They lost two of their calves to sickness last winter. He's interested in buying ours. As pets," he reassured when she almost protested that the neighbors tended to butcher their cows for the table.

"I know a trip to Paris is necessary. I do want to see Maddie again."

The air felt heavy with things she should say, truths she wanted to confess about how she felt about her baby's father, emotions that rose when remembering how they simply seemed to belong with one another.

Her dad smoothed a palm over the back of her hand. "Is he so terrible, then?"

"Sebastian? No. He's possibly the most wonderful man I've ever known." She knew what her dad alluded to: then why avoid him? "He didn't ask me to marry him. And I didn't expect him to. Nor did I want him to, knowing what it might mean. And after how things went with Lloyd… And Mom deciding to leave…"

"Oh, Lea, you mustn't believe the divorce was anything but meant to be. We talked about this. It was a mutual parting."

"I know, but Mom said she felt confined. And you know how I love my freedom. But also…" Now she was just grasping for excuses. Her heart would never give up the dream of having family.

"Marriage is different for everyone. Your mother and I shared thirty wonderful years.

People change. They grow apart. That doesn't mean you should never give a person a go on the off chance the same might happen. Life is meant to be lived. Live it without looking into the crystal ball and asking about your future. Take a chance!"

She sighed. "Maybe my heart was waiting for that proposal from Sebastian after hearing about the baby. Just so I know it was something he would have considered."

"He's being smart. Maybe even cautious of your heart. If he had asked you right away, I would have been suspicious. Like he was only trying to do the right thing."

"Maybe." What was so wrong with that? Well, everything. At least, as far as she'd decided. "Oh, Dad, this is difficult. I should be focusing on finding a job and a place to live. In less than half a year I'm going to be a family!"

"I can't wait to welcome my grandbaby! Heaven knows, Dahlia will never make me a pops. I think we're going with Pops, yeah?"

"Sounds perfect, Pops. I'm glad you're excited about this. It makes everything feel a little easier in the grander scheme of things."

"Raising children is never easy. It's messy, emotionally trying and downright frustrating at times. But it is also wondrous, joyful, and so worth it."

She tilted her head against his shoulder. "I love you, Dad."

"I promise to love the heck out of my grandbaby. I might even save some space in my heart for the tyke's father, too."

"Sebastian takes up a lot of space," she started to say, but swallowed and couldn't bring herself to finish the last part—*in my heart.*

Her dad pulled her into a hug. "It'll all go as it should, Lea. I promise you that."

Days later

Azalea had asked the taxi driver to drive to the L'Homme Mercier atelier and home office in the 6th arrondissement. She'd considered being dropped off out front, but then she'd decided that walking in with suitcases in hand, looking like the last woman the posh Sebastian Mercier would ever involve himself with, would be bad form. She couldn't do that to him, so she redirected the driver.

A small corner hotel offered an available room. It was literally just a room, like in someone's house, with a basin and a bed and a window that looked toward Notre Dame. She plunked her suitcase on the lumpy bed and went to freshen up in the closet-sized bathroom. The lavender soap made her dizzy, so she tucked it away in a drawer.

She hadn't texted Sebastian to let him know she'd be coming to Paris. He'd texted her over the weeks since he'd left the farm. He hadn't asked after the baby, just sending notes to let her know he was thinking about her.

You are in my thoughts.

I miss your bright eyes.

We dance well together.

She appreciated his careful distance. But it also put dread in her heart.

A very rich and powerful man now held a claim to her unborn child. If she didn't go along with whatever he wished, would he take it away from her? It was a dramatic scenario, but she'd played it over many times. Sebastian had been brought up by a father who had many children, all by mothers he'd never married. Could this baby be the first in a collection that Sebastian would grow just as he'd witnessed his father do? After all, he'd known nothing else.

A terrible thought. But something she needed to have answered while here in Paris.

To look on the plus side, she felt great. The morning sickness had passed, though her aversion to smells had grown. Her appetite had also increased. As had her gut. Though she'd yet to pop out with an apparent baby bulge. So far, her middle had thickened, overwhelming what had once been a slender waist. Not the most appealing shape. She'd begun to wear looser clothing—today a spaghetti-strap sundress—to accommodate the weight gain.

Checking her phone, she vacillated between going for a walk and calling him. Sebastian had given her his home address, which was in the 6th arrondissement. The entry codes, for gosh sakes! But it didn't feel right walking in and making herself at home. Much as part of her felt a certain right to do so. Carrying the man's child, anyone? That did grant her some clout. But no. She wasn't the sort to expect anything of him.

Yet why not? And really, *shouldn't* she expect something? And if not from Sebastian, then certainly she must figure in her own expectations for this strange but curious affair of having the rebound man's baby.

"Such dramatics," she muttered. A chuckle was necessary. She was a rural princess, not some wayward romance heroine desperate to claim her baby's father.

"Maybe a little," she then whispered.

And her heart remained hopeful in response to that realization.

Since it was early, she decided to ring up Maddie. Her girlfriend was hopping a flight tomorrow for Berlin, so they arranged to meet at a café in half an hour. Starting this trip with some friend time was what Azalea required to bolster her courage.

Finding the café with ease, Azalea crossed the street. Maddie, seated at an outside table, waved, gold bracelets clinking. She stood to kiss Azalea on both cheeks as she arrived. "I can't believe you're back in Paris. I wish I'd known sooner. We could have spent more time together. So, what's up?"

Azalea sat and took a sip of the water already at the table. "A lot, Maddie. Are you ready for this?"

Her friend wiggled on her chair and excitedly said, "Always!"

CHAPTER ELEVEN

JUST AS HE was leaving the office for the evening, Sebastian received a text from Zee. She was in Paris. An utter explosion of relief loosened muscles that he hadn't realized he'd been holding tight for…possibly weeks. He texted her back that he was on his way to pick her up.

He'd given much thought to the idea of becoming a father. While it hadn't been something he'd planned, it was also something that he'd sought. Weirdly enough. He'd thought of his baby every day since learning she was pregnant. Most of the time he smiled. A few times he shook his head. Was he even ready to become a father? How to be a good parent when all he knew was…well, it was what he knew.

And now he'd been gifted with the very thing that could catapult him to the win.

But a softer, more caring side of him admonished that he couldn't very well take the baby and run, while seeking another woman to marry him. Azalea did not deserve such cruelty. Yet if she wouldn't marry him, what was he to do? If he made the wrong choice, he could very well lose not only the CEO position, but as well, the only women he desired.

How to have both?

He hadn't come to any sane means to obtain Zee's hand in marriage without offending her morals. Kidnapping, threatening and coercion had only been temporary, ridiculous thoughts. He wasn't that man.

Gently wooing her might work. Could it?

For the first time in his life, he struggled with his feelings for a woman. And that was remarkable to realize. Was this, in fact, for the first time in his life...love?

He'd told Zee he thought he was falling in love with her. But at the time he hadn't known for sure. And he wasn't even sure now. The idea of love excited him. And it worried him.

Love might spoil any plans of gaining control over L'Homme Mercier.

Half an hour later, Sebastian collected Zee and her things, and whisked her off to his place. Now she stood before the massive wall of windows, looking out over the city. The sun wouldn't set for hours, but the hazy day cast a shadow over the sky and silhouetted her before him. He felt as though she were untouchable and yet so down-to-earth. A princess of quaint and chickens but also a goddess of beauty and frolic. Yet he couldn't forget when she'd told him she wasn't sure where life would next lead her. He had a few ideas. But he cautioned himself from over-stepping with her. She was skittish. And right-fully so.

Since returning to Paris from Ambleside he'd had opportunities to date and had refused them all. No woman interested him like Zee did. The idea of proposing to anyone but Zee didn't even fit into his brain. And now there was another reason for him to invest in their relationship.

He agreed with Zee on one point: he did not want his child to be a tool to lever his position in the family drama. That was unfair. And reeked of his own childhood. Not an unpleasant upbringing, but even he could understand it wasn't normal, and most certainly was not in Zee's range of comfort.

"How are you feeling?" he asked as he pulled a bottle of sparkling water from the fridge, then poured them both a glass. "Am I allowed to ask?"

"Of course, you are. We are still…friends." She swallowed.

Unsure about that title? It wasn't what he would label them, and it poked at his heart to hear her declare such. On the other hand, who was he to claim something more? How to navigate this delicate balance between them?

"I'm feeling good. I assume you're asking baby-wise? I had a little morning sickness for the first few months but it's gone. It's just odors that bug me now. Although you smell great. Very subtle. I like it."

"Thank you. I finally got the last remnants of Câlin out by hiring a cleaning crew. Remind me never to attend another perfume party."

He handed her the glass and kissed her cheek. He wanted to hug her and never let her go, but she'd flinched when he'd met her at the hotel. Keeping a bit of distance between them? That killed him. He daren't offer a pinkie hug either. She'd not responded the last time he'd tried that. He'd react to her cues.

"I still can't get over how beautiful Paris is," she commented. "It's a cloudy day and still the sky looks like a painting. Is that Notre Dame over there, with the scaffolding climbing the structure?"

"It is. Under repair following the fire a few years ago. Though soon it will be complete."

If she intended to pussyfoot around the subject that he'd not been able to stop thinking about the past few weeks, he would pull out his hair. But he reminded himself to give her some measure, and to allow her the lead.

"I'm sorry it took so long," she said. "I mean, to come here. Dad got back a few weeks ago and I told him about the baby. He's over the moon to become a grandpa. Pops is what he's decided the baby will call him. Diane, his girlfriend, is excited as well. She's been doting on me."

"Doting is good, yes?" Some things got lost in translation.

"It involves lots of stories about when she was a mother, shopping for baby things, and stories about how to breastfeed properly and select the best pram. So, yes, very good." She set down the water and splayed her hands before her. "So. We need to talk."

"I don't intend to make talking to me a hardship, Zee. Are you so against the idea that we now have a connection? You called us merely friends. I thought we got along so well."

"We did. We do. It's just…everything has changed." She sat on the sofa that faced the windows and patted the cushion beside her. "First tell me how things are going for you at work. You had a meeting you had to get home to? How did that go?"

"It was for next year's spring line. All signed, sealed and sent to the tailor. And work is always a pleasure for me."

"I know that about you. That's why I also know how important it is that you win the CEO position."

He sat next to her and took her hand, kissing the back of it. The softness of her skin brought him instantly back to her farm, sitting on the porch, watching the sun beam across the pond. With chickens. An odd moment to remember, since it should be the very last thing that he cared to repeat, the country retreat part. And yet, if Zee were beside him, would he be comfortable spending the rest of his days living such a scenario?

"I don't want to talk about work, Zee. I've done a lot of thinking these few weeks. About us."

"I don't think there can be an us."

He turned abruptly to search her gaze. She looked down, avoiding his nudging desire to find the truth in her eyes. "Zee?"

"It all comes down to that stupid competition. I won't be a part of it. It's unfair to me."

"First, I haven't asked you to marry me. And second, I'm not so insensitive. You mustn't believe I would use you in such a manner, Zee. You mean too much to me."

"That's lovely to hear, but I will never know if you're saying it because it's what I want to hear or if it comes from your heart."

"It comes from my heart. I know we haven't known one another long, but you should know that I am a man of my word. I do not tolerate lies."

"I think I know that." She sighed and leaned against the cushions, closing her eyes. The hazy light emphasized her freckles. "I can do this on my own. I just need to find a job. Get a little place in London—"

"But you told me London is too big and noisy."

"It is, but it may be the only option. And Dahlia has already started scoping out potential flats for me."

"A London flat is expensive. And you have no income. Zee, I don't want you to sacrifice your comfort for the necessity of earning an income. And who will take care of the baby?"

"I'll hire a sitter. Day care is also an option. Both are…well…" She winced.

"What you can't say is that they are expensive. So you'll work to pay someone to watch our child while you work…to pay for childcare? Sounds like running in circles to me. You don't want to do that, Zee. I know you. Your best friend is a cow. You thrive when you are wandering the grass barefoot and dancing with the flowers. I can't imagine you'd want to raise a child in London."

She shook her head. "Not really. But it's a place

to start. I can find a job at a florist, or maybe a supermarket."

He cringed. "You, a supermarket clerk? Absolutely not. Such a menial job would extinguish your bright light."

"A person can find joy in any task if they look for it. Even shelving canned tomatoes. Sebastian, I'd do anything for my baby. I want to give it the best life."

"The best for our baby is to have its mother there for it. As well as its father. I want to be a part of my child's life," he insisted. "I need to be a part of his life."

"His?"

"I'm sure of it." He smiled. "I have a feeling. But I won't force you to allow me into his life. I don't want to be that man who controls people with his money. I want to be in his life because you want me there. And Zee, I will take care of you. No matter what you decide. I'll find a place for you to live. Or you find the perfect place and then I'll finance it. You'll never want for anything. You simply need to enjoy being a mother."

"No matter what I decide? Like I have options? Sebastian, this is one choice I know isn't a mistake. I'm having this baby."

"Of course, you are. I'm sorry, I didn't mean to imply there were any other options."

"I didn't plan for it, but now that it's here..." she patted her stomach "...inside me, I'm actually excited about this little bean. Boy or girl, I'll be happy either way."

Sebastian wished she could be as excited about inviting him to share in the baby's life. But then, he hadn't given her any reason to do so. Proposing felt wrong. She'd flee, insisting he wanted to marry her to become CEO. It wouldn't be like that. Maybe a little like that? If he wasn't even certain himself, then he could hardly be certain with her. But he could understand how she would think. So taking care of her was his only option.

For now.

To win her over and change the course of his future was the question. Because winning Azalea and his baby meant forfeiting the CEO position.

He kissed her cheek and nuzzled his head aside hers. Raising a hand to place over her stomach, he stopped before touching her. "May I?"

"Uh...yes." She took his hand and laid it over her stomach. She didn't appear pregnant, though perhaps she'd filled out a bit? "The baby doesn't start noticeably moving around for a few more weeks. I read about it online. I'm about four months according to my doctor."

"I'm pleased you've seen a doctor. I'll cover all your medical bills. Will you allow that?"

"The prenatal visit was free, and most of the rest is, including the midwife, but there will be expenses..."

"I'll make sure you get a card to use for any and all expenses. Medical, baby supplies, food, anything, Zee. You've only to ask."

"You know you can't buy my baby with the slash of a credit card."

Sebastian gaped at her. "How can you say such a thing? I would never."

A curious anger forced him to stand and stride into the kitchen where he grabbed the bottle of sparkling water. He was not buying her baby because—it was *his* baby, too! How dare she use such an accusation to repel him? He had as much right to watch their child grow up as she did. Why was it the woman always got the key role and more say in what would happen with the baby? It wasn't right.

He was still embracing this news about being a father, but more and more he was excited about it. And he wanted to share those feelings with her. He wanted to hear the stories about the best prams and how to survive the sleepless nights that would come with fatherhood. He wanted to be there for his child's first smile, his first words, his first toddle across the yard.

"I'm sorry," she said quietly. "This is an unusual situation to navigate. If not a little weird. Don't you think so?"

He took a swig directly from the bottle. "I do think it's out of the usual. Though not by my family's standards. It would be easier if we were…" At the very least, in one another's lives. In the same country. On the same page. "Am I to believe you don't want to be my girlfriend, then?"

"I…wasn't aware that title was on the table. I've only ever considered us lovers. Friends. Sebastian, I don't even live in Paris!"

"But do you live in Ambleside? Not for much longer."

She shrugged and gestured dismissively. "I will probably have to move before the leaves drop from the trees."

"Which is fast upon us. What about a cozy little town on the outskirts of Paris? Something wooded and with cobblestones and cows and chickens?"

She laughed, then looked up at him, as if realizing he was not joking. She had her dreams of being a princess; he could dream, too. Yet he wasn't quite sure what the dream of his future looked like. He was winging it. Trying to please her and not make a wrong step.

"So that's a possibility," he boldly decided.

"Good to know. As I've once said about you, you teeter between village life and big-city life."

She agreed with a nod. "A happy medium would be perfect."

"At the very least, will you stay in Paris for a while? Grant me some time with you? Let me romance you as I've wanted to do every day we've been apart."

"I do like how you romance me."

"I think you're talking about the sex part."

"All your sex parts are quite lovely."

Was that a blush he felt heating his neck? "I'll work half days so I can spend all my time with you. We'll have a grand time."

"Until?"

He wasn't sure what she wanted him to say. He didn't know where this relationship was headed, or how it would get there. But if he could win another day, week, or more with her, then he'd snatch it and honor it as something precious.

"Until you need to seriously start wife hunting," she said.

Sebastian clutched the neck of the bottle. That was a sticking point she wasn't able to get beyond. Something that he should not overlook. Life had delivered him an interesting curve. He could follow it and see where it led him or try to straighten it back on course.

He wasn't at all sure which was the better choice. And really, what *was* his course?

"Should we make a deal not to talk about wife hunting or baby heirs?" she asked. "Just have some fun for a few days?"

He nodded. But it wouldn't be simple fun. It could mean the start to something grand.

Or the beginning of unbearable heartbreak.

CHAPTER TWELVE

Days later

THE LIMO PULLED to the curb and Sebastian leaned over to kiss Azalea. “Ready?”

She inhaled and said, “Give me a minute.”

“We can sit here as long as you like. Are you nervous to meet my friends?”

Yes, she was. She had spent the afternoon shopping for the perfect dress to wear tonight. Not too fancy, not so country bumpkin as her favorite floral dresses were. She’d landed on a simple white linen dress that did not have a tucked waistline. Red sandals were a necessity since lately her feet were swollen. So much for doing this pregnancy gracefully. Everything was growing larger. Puffy. Although she’d take the swollen breasts since they did now make her look like a B-cup.

She was confident she looked passable, but the key now was to not come off as uneducated or a farm girl. Lloyd’s words had embedded themselves into her soul. She wanted to ignore what he'd said, but right now it was hard not to feel those words wrap around her like a bold red flag. Surely Sebastian's friends were rich and elite and maybe even snobbish?

"A little nervous?" she offered.

"You mustn't worry. They will love you. And they are not pretentious. If anything, they laugh at me when I have a model on my arm. They are always telling me to find a woman of substance and elan."

"And look what you've come up with. The chicken lady from England."

He laughed heartily. "That's a good one. I will have to tell them that one."

"No, don't! Sebastian, please, I just want to make a good impression."

He kissed her. Each time they connected, no matter how briefly, it fortified her courage a little more. "The only one you have to impress is me, and you've already succeeded on that front. Come on. You'll be surprised at how down-to-earth they are."

She nodded. Just the fact he'd arranged for her to meet his friends had to mean something. Had he told them about the baby? She hoped not. It was too big a topic to get into with people she didn't know. Right now, she just wanted to get through the evening. And perhaps learn a little more about Sebastian in the process.

They got out and entered a cozy restaurant walled with black steel and blue furnishings. A circular fireplace at the center was viewable by all the tables. Sebastian held her hand firmly, and when they arrived at a half-circle booth, three men and two women greeted her warmly.

"Azalea is not fluent in French, so tonight we will speak English for her, please?" he asked.

"Of course!" they all chimed.

An hour into drinks—nonalcoholic for Azalea and Sebastian—and a round of appetizers and desserts, Azalea had relaxed and was laughing along with everyone else as they went round the table telling tales about their adventures with Sebastian. From boating excursions in Marseilles that resulted in a broken-down engine that left them stranded for hours, to college lacrosse days when he'd led the team to a championship. They genuinely cared about him, and he was right when he'd told her they were not pretentious. She did not feel as though they were judging her. And she relaxed even more, her thigh hugging his, her head tilting onto his shoulder occasionally.

The past few days had been adventurous, visiting the Paris sights, afternoons wandering lush city parks, and evenings spent making love and staring out the window at the city lights. As well, carrying the weight of the situation between her and Sebastian, which had begun to sink in deeply. There was no easy resolution to what they'd created between them. She was thankful no one had brought up "the rebound baby." It was still her and Sebastian's secret.

When she yawned, she tried to disguise it behind her hand, but Clemente, the gorgeous redhead with silver dangle earrings, noticed and suggested that they end the night. "I'm as tired as Azalea looks," she said sweetly. "How about we split the tab?"

"No, I've got it." Sebastian gestured to the waiter to bring the check. "It's been a marvelous evening. *Merci, mon amies!*"

"And thank you for going out of your way and speaking English for me," Azalea added. "That was very kind."

"Not a problem." Charles, who worked for Sebastian's competition as a marketing exec, said with a pat to the back of her hand. "You're adorable, Zee. We hope to see you again, and soon."

"*Oui*, very soon," echoed out as everyone rose and began to leave with kisses to cheeks.

Consumed by a whirlwind of cheek busses, she finally stood in Sebastian's arms out front of the restaurant. "I like your friends." She sighed and sank against his chest.

"I'm glad. They very much liked you."

"Thank you for not telling them I'm pregnant. I'm not sure how to deal with that announcement yet."

"No worries." He held up his hand, pinkie out.

She met his hug with her pinkie, glad for the secret code that meant to her that they did care for one another and no matter what happened, she trusted he would treat her well.

"Shall I also keep it a secret this weekend when we do supper with my family?"

"Your family?" Suddenly Azalea's throat went dry. Her heart pounded. "Oh, I don't know about meeting the family, Sebastian."

"Why not? We get together once a month, all of us, including all of the moms and girlfriends and kids. They'll love you as much as my friends do."

"But I thought you said your family wouldn't approve of me?"

He winced. "That was a crass thing to say. I regret it. I realize it doesn't matter to me what my family thinks of anyone in my life. All that matters is how I feel when with you. We're not trying to impress anyone, are we? Let's go and have a good time and you can meet Philippe and my dad. Roman has been working with a speech therapist. He still has trouble enunciating words but he has a manner of getting his point across."

"I'm glad to hear he's recovering. But seriously, you may not think it a big deal, but this is going to be my first impression on them. I might need something different to wear."

"You have the card I gave you. Buy what you need."

"It's generous of you to give me whatever I want but I could take advantage and buy a car or something."

"If it makes you happy, it makes me happy. Besides, what good is it to have money if you do not use it to buy things you enjoy?"

"Oh, mercy, you will corrupt me."

"And I intend to enjoy every minute of it."

Making love to Sebastian was the best feeling in the world. Besides taking off her bra after a long day. Nothing could compete with that feeling. But she'd never tell him he had competition. And that her mind wandered to silly things like undergarments after she'd just climaxed—for the second time—bothered Azalea.

Because after the bra she started thinking about his family. She didn't want to meet the family! Did she really have to? But of course, if she was to have Sebastian's baby, she should probably assess the relative situation. On her side the issue was easy enough. One grandpa and grandma and their respective partners. On Sebastian's side it was the one grandpa and… how many grandmothers? She'd lost count. And would they be called step-grandmothers?

Kisses to her spine stirred her from her mad-making thoughts and she rolled over to snuggle against Sebastian's chest. Heated vanilla, cedar and saltiness scented his skin. She nuzzled closer and licked him. "You are a talented man."

"And you are a vocal woman. I love when you climax."

She smiled against his skin. "You're not so quiet yourself."

"Fortunately, I own the whole top floor of this building, so we can be as loud as we care to be."

With that permission, she let out a long and bellowing call that ended in a giggle.

"Is that so?" He tickled her ribs in punishment.

Her laughter turned to shrieks and kicks and then she collapsed in a huffing sigh of relief as his tickles turned to kisses from neck to breasts, to stomach. Gentle and reverent, he took his time covering her entire growing belly. Then he pressed his ear against her stomach.

"Can I help you name him?" he asked.

She'd not yet given thought to names. Hadn't

any favorites. And how he guessed it was a boy was cute, but she'd not gotten confirmation during the ultrasound on the sex.

"Of course, you can. As long as it's not Clifford or Harry."

"What's wrong with Harry?"

"That would remind me of my lost love," she said with a dramatic tone.

"Do tell?"

"When I was in primary school I intended to marry Harry Marks. He once gave a report on how he wanted to be a prince when he grew up. At the time I didn't realize you had to be born into the title. Anyway, you know about my aspirations to princess-hood. Alas, the last I heard, Harry works as a bartender in the West End."

"Alas," he mocked gently.

"Oh, come on! I could have been a princess."

"You already are a rural princess, Zee. And I'll fight Harry any day to win your regard."

She assessed him in the pale beam of moonlight that shone across the head of the bed. "You did offer to punch the photographer that night you rescued me. You must be quite the brawler."

"I did punch him."

She gaped at him. "What?"

"I brought back the dress and made sure he understood he'd done wrong."

"Seriously?"

He shrugged.

"Wow. You're my knight in shining menswear. Your suit is your armor."

"I suppose it is." He kissed her belly and tugged her against him, her back to his chest, and nuzzled his face into her hair. "I'm falling in love with you, Zee. And I'm not using the word *think* this time around. This time I can feel it right here, in my entire being."

His words sounded so real. Just what she wanted to hear from him.

"Don't be mad?" he added.

"Of course not." And yet, she wasn't happy.

And why she wasn't happy astounded her. Because the man of her dreams had just confessed his love to her. Or almost love. And he wanted her to have everything that would make her life, and the life of her child, perfect. She should be dancing with joy. Over the moon. Wearing that princess crown with pride.

Yet how to get over the self-imposed caution that would not allow her to believe Sebastian was only in this for the CEO position?

CHAPTER THIRTEEN

TEN DAYS HAD passed since Azalea had come to Paris. Puttering around the neighborhood, slipping in and out of the trendy shops, and browsing Sebastian's home while he was away at work felt like the most normal thing in the world. There was plenty to keep her busy, from exploring the parks and cafés, to exploring the elegant suits in his closet and laughing over his meticulously ordered fridge. Yes, there were hues of wine and each bottle was arranged in order from pale to dark. As well, the cheeses were in alphabetical order!

She'd not even considered when she would return to Ambleside. Though she had thought about finding a job. She could look into teaching English as a second language, or even apply at one of the florists on the main strip hugging the river, using her English as an attribute considering all the tourist business that must demand a command of the language.

"Possible," she muttered as she scrolled through a website that sold baby furniture and clothing.

She preferred the plain pinewood furniture and simple clothing that wasn't frilly or the declarative pink or blue. Her toddler would amble through the grass barefoot and chase butterflies in whatever color inspired her that day.

"He has to," she said with the dream swelling in her heart. "That's how I want to raise a child. Free and wild. Respectful and prone to common sense."

She would definitely homeschool. But that was a lofty dream for a penniless, pregnant woman who had no home or job.

Sebastian's offer to pay for everything was not to be disregarded. Which was why she'd accepted the credit card he'd handed her. She wasn't going to refuse it on some arrogant moral ground that she was too good for charity. Heck, he was the father. He could chip in to raise their child. However, she did want to make her own way as well. A happy medium must be achieved. Because while she was living it up, enjoying the luxurious life in a swanky Parisian penthouse, eating at exclusive restaurants and buying fabulous clothes, she didn't want to take advantage of Sebastian. Nor did her aesthetics require such swank. Not all the time, anyway.

Simple things. A simple life. With a side of Weekend Parisian Princess added to the mix?

The thought made her smile.

"How to incorporate Sebastian Mercier into my simple plan?" she murmured. "And at the same time give an inch and occasionally slide into his world?"

Could she incorporate him into her life in a meaningful way that would allow her to accept his need to keep a wife? No. If he married, or even if he dated someone else while keeping her on the side as his family, the way all the Mercier men seemed to keep women, Azalea was absolutely sure she did not want a part of that.

But convincing him *not* to go for the CEO position would be unfair to him. He wanted that job. He had plans, dreams for the company. She couldn't deny him that win by insisting he not marry another.

It could be as simple as telling him they should get married. It would give him the win. Could it ever be a real marriage?

Maybe?

"I only want it if it's real."

"Hey, Dad, how's it going on the farm?"

"Casual, as usual, with a side of packing and tossing all the junk we don't need. How's it with you and Sebastian? Are you working things out?"

Azalea bit her lip. She never lied to her dad. And really, even she wasn't sure they had worked things out, so a straight yes or no couldn't apply.

"Lea, sweetie, you've got to get things straight with him."

"I'm not sure what is straight for me, Dad. I'm still working this out in my heart, if you can understand that."

"I do. You don't want to be treated any lesser than what you deserve. Nor do I wish that for you. You know Diane and I will support whatever decision you make."

"I know you will. So, what's up?"

"I just called to let you know we've had some offers for the property."

"Dad, that's wonderful."

Was it? Azalea's heart sank. Such good news would allow her dad to take the next step. But she felt some panic in that it felt as if her life, her very roots, had just been torn up and were dangling like dirt clumps above a hole in the earth. Her escape to the farm would soon be gone. Then where would she go?

"What about Stella and Daisy?"

"They sold two days ago."

"What?" He'd just up and sold her best friend?

"You knew I was selling them, Lea. The neighbor is going to pick them up in a few days. He's promised not to eat them, I swear."

That sounded so not reassuring.

"The hens are..." He exhaled heavily and she knew that meant he and Diane would be feasting on chicken for the next few weeks. "It's going well, sweetie."

"I'm glad for you, Dad. Though I wish I could be there to send off Stella." She slid a hand over her not too round belly. Still, she was proud of it. "I have a feeling no matter where life takes me and this little one, it may involve a cow."

Her dad laughed. "Sure you don't want to buy the farm from me? There's still time."

Not that she could afford such a thing. Would it be possible? No, it wouldn't be fair to her dad to work up an arrangement to keep something that she loved, yet also felt would keep her from moving on. She needed to forge her own life.

"If you're selling at fire sale prices, sure."

Another laugh. "Let me know when you've plans to return. I'll drive to London to pick you up."

"Thanks, Dad. I'm not sure how much longer I'll stay. I'll ring you when I do. Love you!"

She hung up and tossed the phone to the comfy sofa and walked up to the window to look out over Paris. The sun was bright and tendrils of some vine twisting about a nearby tree snaked toward the window. The city of lights was so pretty. And here in Sebastian's home, it felt not quite so busy and hustling as London had to her. Still, it wasn't exactly her style. Even if it was home to a man she couldn't imagine pushing out of her life.

Sebastian's trajectory and hers were not aimed toward one another. His life was here in Paris. Hers was…not here. And there was nothing left for her in Ambleside after the farm was sold.

The door opened and Sebastian breezed in, as was his habit. Even after a full day at the office he always seemed light on his feet, his smile seeking hers. If a person's eyes could speak his screamed happiness. It was difficult to sulk when in his presence.

Azalea sailed toward him and he swept her into an embrace that suddenly turned into a full-on, dance-floor dip. She let out a hoot, and he pulled her upright to kiss her. Her Frenchman's five-o'clock shadow tickled her skin, perking her nipples and zinging desire through her system. As their kiss deepened, they swayed to an unsung melody backed up by the timpani of their heartbeats.

When she came up for air, she asked, "What was that for?"

He shrugged. "The best part of my day is coming home to find you here, smiling at me."

"I was thinking much the same."

"Another dip!" He spun her before the window and when she swirled back to him, he bowed her low. "Do you think we could qualify for that dancing show on the TV?"

"Why not?" He spun her upright and she landed in his secure embrace and they kissed again.

Everything was perfect. And everything was wrong. His kisses only managed to distract her from the more serious stakes.

"Can we make this work?" he asked.

"I'm not sure."

"Do you want to make it work?"

"Honestly? I want to, but I'm also cautious because I don't want my heart to get broken."

"I would never do anything to hurt you, Zee. Or our baby." He spread a palm across her stomach. "I think you've got a little belly?"

"Don't remind me. It's not so much a belly as a full spread. I feel like a lump."

"A beautiful lump." He bent to kiss her stomach. Feeling him there, paying respect to their child, made her question if she were being too protective of her heart. Should she give him a chance?

"Are you ready for tomorrow night? The dinner with my family?"

"Oh." Her consternation switched to panic. "I haven't found a dress yet."

"We'll go shopping in the morning. Don't worry, Zee, I'll hold your hand." He clasped hers and kissed it. "It won't be so terrible. Dad is more quiet than usual. The girlfriends are all a bit materialistic and focused on fashion and jewels. Like those housewife shows on the television."

Azalea laughed. "And your brother. Will he have a date?"

"Not sure. I haven't spoken to Philippe for a few weeks. But we do try to show up at these family soirees with a date."

"To show the other you're committed to the competition?"

"This—us—is not competition," he said. "I've found the perfect woman. And she's already told me she won't marry me, so I must suffice with merely adoring her for the rest of my life."

"Don't be foolish, Sebastian. You wouldn't give up the CEO position to stare at me as I grow fatter and my fingers and toes swell to sausages."

"Honestly? It's something I wrestle with daily."

"I hope the CEO position wins."

"Really?" He studied her with that perceptively delving gaze that always brought her to her knees. "You don't want me to choose you?"

"I want you to be happy. And the CEO position would make you happy."

"It would. But *you* also make me happy."

"You can't have both."

He sighed. "No, apparently not."

"Besides, don't you know happiness is an inside job? Only you can make yourself happy. And if you're not happy on your own, then it doesn't matter if another person comes into your life and makes an attempt to create that happiness."

"Profound," he said. "Are you happy?"

"I am. Mostly. I would be much happier if I had definite future plans, but I feel as though things will work themselves out."

"So you don't require me in your life to be happy?"

Answer truthfully, her conscience nudged.

Azalea shrugged and shook her head. "But you are a nice bonus."

"The bonus guy. How utterly romantic."

"Don't take it the wrong way. I adore you, Sebastian. And… I really do hope things can work for us. But I'm not going to make plans for something that I feel isn't a sure thing."

"What about life *is* a sure thing?"

"Not much." Her father had said much the same to her. *Life is meant to be lived. Go off and live it!*

"Well, we'll see how things go, eh?"

Yes, they did like to dance around making

a final decision on this situation. And she was fine with that. Because Azalea sensed any decision would result in heartbreak for one, if not both of them.

"No matter what happens between us?" he said. "I am going to create a stipend for you and my child. You'll never want for anything, Zee. I promise you that."

"Oh. Well." That was very generous beyond the credit card he'd already given her. But not so surprising, knowing Sebastian for the kind and generous man he was.

"Tell me you'll accept?"

It would help her in the interim until she could really figure things out, decide what the future looked like for her with a child, and maybe or maybe not the child's father.

She nodded. "Thank you. But I only need a little help until I get my life on track—"

The kiss he often employed to stop her from rambling senselessly never failed to be successful. And to shift Azalea from brain mode to soft and accepting heart mode. Could she seriously imagine life without Sebastian's kisses?

"You'll have an account forever, Zee. That's how it's going to go. Like it or not. Now, I ordered food on the way home. I'm going to wash up. If the bell rings, answer it!"

He strolled down the hallway, leaving her

feeling floaty from his kiss, but at the same time she could feel the chain tighten about her ankle that bound her to the floor. His floor. His chain. His money. She'd become one of those women his father collected, mothers of his children the patriarch wasn't willing to commit to.

Would Sebastian feel he could direct her future, and that of her child's, because he was financing it? She didn't want that.

Had accepting his offer been a mistake?

She shimmied off a creeping tightness in her shoulders and shook out her hands. "No, it'll work. It has to."

While Zee was in the shower, Sebastian washed the dinner dishes. Night hugged the windows with a glint of moonshine across the glass and an ambient pink glow from the city's neon. The neighborhood was old and quiet, but the heart of Paris was always present no matter where one lived or stood within the city. Lights, river, history. This was his home. He loved it. Couldn't imagine living anywhere else.

Now that he was to become a father, he had some hard choices to face. He wanted to see his son raised in Paris, or at the very least, France. His child must speak French, and of course English. He would know his family and their history—with some careful edits and alterations regarding what a family really was. And that meant he should consider going traditional and marrying his child's mother. Bring him up in a nuclear family surrounded by those who loved him.

Yet how to convince Zee of that? Surely she must want the best for their child? And she couldn't believe denying her son his father would be for the better. He knew she didn't believe that.

Was he ready to make the commitment and propose to her? He'd twice already made a proposal. Hell, he even had the ring. But those times had meant nothing more than winning a competition. They hadn't been based on love, respect or even like.

It was different with Zee. As much as she teased that he couldn't possibly love her—and perhaps he was mistaken, for the only kind of love he knew was that which he'd experienced from his family—he did feel a deep respect and attachment to her. And what better basis for starting a family, something formed from friendship, laughter and passion? All of which had nothing to do with the competition. He didn't want it to be associated with the infernal contest. Because that detail was the one thing that kept Azalea from seeing him.

Could she ever see him for his own man? Someone who had not followed in the footsteps of a pleasure-seeking rogue who could not commit to his children's mothers?

Dinner with his family would either cement Zee's opinion or change it. And he wasn't feeling very positive about which way that pendulum would swing.

CHAPTER FOURTEEN

WATCHING THE SUNRISE from the balcony that wrapped around Sebastian's penthouse, a soft blanket wrapped about her naked body, Azalea felt as if she existed inside of a dream. She had crept out of bed, leaving Sebastian sprawled on his back, arms out and legs wide, still asleep. The guy was a master at the unconcerned sleep. She loved it.

Now she leaned against the ornate wrought iron railing. The city was quiet, and a foggy heaviness sweatered her with the heat of August. It felt like a hug from Paris. Seeming to rise from the dash of rose light that hugged the horizon, the Sacré-Coeur Basilica, far on the Right Bank, pierced the gold sky with its bleach-white spires. Closer, wearing scaffolds like intricate lace, Notre Dame announced to all that she would not be taken down, no matter the strife she endured. Below on the sidewalk, a woman in sleek jogging wear ran by, earbuds depriving her of the peaceful morning.

It wasn't like rising to Big Bruce's call and then wandering through a meadow barefoot, each step stirring wild and earthy scents, but Azalea wouldn't neglect this moment. This was the Paris she could manage in her life. Quiet, beautiful, something out of a postcard. But give it a few more hours and the rush and hubbub would change her mind.

Dinner with the family tonight. A dreadful clutch at her heart forced a swallow. But really, she was a grown woman. She could do this. A few hours seated before the eyes of a klatch of snooty girlfriends, a virtually speechless and likely judging father, and the brother who viewed Sebastian as his greatest competition?

What could possibly go wrong?

Smirking at the disaster scenarios that deluged her brain, she shook them all away. This night would go well. And she did want to meet the family that had influenced Sebastian's life. They were going to be her child's relatives. Whether or not they were included in that child's life was a matter for another day. First, she had to gather basic intel and check out the gene pool.

"Zee," Sebastian called from the bed. She'd left the balcony door open. "Come back to bed."

"It's perfect out here." She remained by the railing, despite his wanting moan that seemed to vibrate through her erogenous zones.

A glance over her shoulder saw he'd rolled to his side, back away from the morning light, derriere exposed. Now, that was a sight she couldn't resist. And it gave fun definition to the word *manhandling.*

Enough city-gazing. Time to put her hands on that.

Sebastian tugged at the violet silk tie that added some color to his simple black velvet smoking jacket and trousers. From last year's summer line, the violet silk was tied in a trinity knot. The single button on the jacket was a Louis d'Or minted in the sixteenth century. The gold coin added a touch of flair to the look. He felt comfortable. On trend. Fashionably right on the mark.

Roman Mercier appreciated his sons' attention to even the smallest fashion details. Rather, he expected such diligence. Sebastian could recall, as a child, watching his dad dress and being tutored in the correct arm length for the various dinner, smoking or tuxedo jackets. Proper shirt styles for all suits, jackets and occasions. How to pair shoes with trousers, and what colors went with what seasons. Styling the perfect suit was like breath to Sebastian. It was his second language, even before English, which he got to use so much lately with Zee.

Another tug wasn't necessary to loosen the

tie, but rather readjust it slightly. It was being stubborn. Hmm… Ties never gave him bother, so why…

With a wince, he realized he was nervous about tonight.

He'd wanted to accompany Zee on her afternoon shopping adventure to select a suitable dress, but a call from the office concerning an emergency fitting for a visiting celebrity hadn't allowed such. And when she'd asked him if he didn't trust her fashion sense, those big blue eyes had lured him to tell her of course he did.

He hadn't lied. Maybe a little. But he'd also the sense to encourage her to be herself. And she had found the perfect dress. This evening his rural princess teased big-city casual chic.

Flicking off the lights and spinning out to retrieve his date by the front door, he took the elevator with her to street level.

Now, sitting next to him in the back of the limo, Zee smoothed at the white fabric splashed with florals. It was cut just above her knees and hugged her figure with a sweetheart neckline. Her soft blond hair was done in loose waves that framed her face and the red lip matched the flowers on the dress. Sweet yet elegant.

Now, if he could just get his head straight on how to handle the situation of her pregnancy.

It could mean the win to him. If they married. That was the calculating way to look at things.

Yet a softer, more heartfelt, side of him simply wanted to do right by her and make her happy. And to be a father to the baby that he had helped create. He couldn't imagine not being involved in the upbringing of his child, unplanned or not. But that way also looked exactly like the path of Roman Mercier. And that did not suit him either.

Realizing she'd given his hand a squeeze, Sebastian then noticed the limo had stopped. "Right. We're here. You ready for this?"

Her nervous nod told him so much. Honestly, he shared her butterflies. His mother could be judgmental at times. *Merde...* All the time.

"I've got you," he promised. "We can do this together."

She exhaled heavily. "Yep. Together."

The Mercier family met monthly in a private top-floor room at an elite four-star restaurant in the 8th arrondissement. The owner was a former lover of Roman Mercier's, though she'd not produced a child and therefore didn't qualify for the family dinners. Sebastian had lost count of all the women who had passed through his father's life over the years. It would be madness to try and keep a tally.

Once out of the elevator, they were greeted by

a friendly hostess, and he accepted a drink from the waiter who offered wine and champagne. He suggested sparkling water for Azalea, and the waiter dashed off to get that.

"Ah! There are my baby brothers." He walked up to greet them.

"Sebastian, so good to see you!" A woman in an elegant black silk gown walked alongside the nanny dressed in plain black linen, who toted a baby on her hip. In a stroller sat another rambunctious baby.

She bussed Sebastian on both cheeks, then eyed Azalea. "And who have we here?"

"Elaine, this is Azalea Grace. My…girlfriend." He smiled at her and she affirmed the label by returning the smile. "Zee, this is Elaine Desmauliers. And this here—" He bent to the baby in the stroller. "Is Henri?"

He got a nod from the nanny that his guess had been right. The twins were only nine months old and were always dressed identically. Tonight, they sported black onesies with a designer logo in leather applique across the bellies. Who could tell the dark-haired sprites apart?

"Hey, Henri." He waggled the baby's toe, clad in matching designer socks. "How's my little brother?"

"So nice to meet you," Azalea said to Elaine and offered her hand to shake.

Elaine leaned in and bussed her cheeks. "Lovely, *cherie*. What a pretty dress."

Sebastian picked up on the snide tone and returned his attention to Zee. He slid an arm around her waist and tugged her close. "There's never a moment Zee is not the most beautiful woman in the room."

Elaine's elegantly tweezed eyebrow lifted. He had seen the bills come through the L'Homme Mercier accounts that authorized twenty thousand euros monthly for the woman's coiffure and wellness spa expenses. "Well, well. Have you found the one?"

Sebastian smirked. "I'll leave Zee to decide whether she has successfully captured me. But we must get on to the dining room. How is Father tonight?"

He hooked his arm in Zee's and led her as Elaine took up his other arm. Behind them, the nanny followed, pushing the stroller.

"He is doing well," Elaine said. "His inability to get some words out frustrates him, but he is easier to understand every day. He's changed, Sebastian. You will remark it, I'm sure."

"Changed? How so?"

"He's softening. More so even than he did following the first stroke." She patted his hand and looked up at him.

He read the success in her eyes. She would

love to be the one woman who finally procured a ring on her finger from Roman Mercier. Sebastian doubted that would happen, but he wished her luck, if only for Henri's and Charles's sakes.

They entered the dining room through elegant Art Deco stained glass doors. Zee's grip on his arm tightened as they stopped before the long dining table. The rest of the family was already seated. All looked up to take them in.

Sebastian leaned in to whisper at Zee's ear, "Ready?"

"As I'll ever be."

After introductions, and some initial questions from each of the family members regarding Sebastian and Azalea's relationship, everyone seemed to settle and sniff at their wine and poke at the hors d'oeuvres.

The room was amazing, featuring more of the Art Deco stained glass, lots of dark woods, gold flatware—was it *real* gold?—and a bottle of champagne so large Azalea wasn't sure anyone would even be able to lift it to pour.

Her nerves did not settle. Maybe her upset stomach was more baby-related than nerves. She hoped not. Now would not be a good time to start delivering on the vomiting she'd avoided during morning sickness. So she sipped water constantly, then realized that must look suspicious. Pushing the goblet forward on the table she clasped her hands on her lap.

Roman Mercier's girlfriends were all glamorous, and there wasn't a single one of the three of them—Elaine, Angelique and Cecile—who did not look artificially enhanced with breasts that defied gravity or cheekbones and lips that plumped just a bit too unnaturally. But on the surface, they were kind and, beyond catching their assessing gazes of her perfectly plain dress—spangles and rhinestones seemed *de rigueur*—Azalea didn't feel like a piece of overcooked meat that none of the elites wanted to touch.

Yet.

Philippe, the brother—son of Cecile—who shared Sebastian's dark hair and gray-blue eyes, but was stockier and more built with thick biceps, eyed her suspiciously. He also had a girlfriend sitting alongside him, not as uber-plumped but certainly working the sequins and glamorous hairstyle, and with eyebrows that defined perfection. He kept a keen eye on Azalea. Was Philippe sizing up his chances at being first to the marriage stipulation of the competition? What might it do to him if he learned his brother had successfully completed the "produce an heir" portion of the race to the win?

And the fact Sebastian introduced her as his girlfriend both annoyed and excited her. They hadn't agreed on such a designation. Sure, they'd spent the last days with one another as if they were in a relationship. Had chatted with his friends as if they were a couple. *Did* that make her his girlfriend? She loved the *idea* of being Sebastian's girlfriend.

Though certainly carrying the man's baby did give the girlfriend label some credence.

Oh, Azalea, stop analyzing! Just try to enjoy this night. The sooner it will be done.

And then later at his place they could discuss the way they would label their relationship. Because it did need a label. For her sanity.

The woman seated on the other side of the table from her, next to Sebastian's father, was Angelique, Sebastian's mom. Dazzling in pale pink beaded chiffon, the woman eyed Azalea covertly through long false lashes. Wicked red nails caressed a champagne goblet. Sebastian had to have told her a little about his date. Was the woman musing that Azalea was just a country bumpkin and how dare she insinuate herself into her son's life? Most likely.

When the main course was served, Azalea took some solace in being able to eat and not make eye contact with anyone. Sebastian reached under the table and gave her thigh a squeeze. He leaned in and whispered, "Still good?"

She nodded. Yes, as long as he was by her side, she was good. So far, none of the women had scratched out her eyes. Not that they had reason to. It was the competitive brother who worried her. And at that moment, Philippe stood, gesturing for everyone to silence.

Azalea met Sebastian's gaze and he shrugged, indicating he had no idea what was to come.

"Family," Philippe began, "I have exciting news I must share before the desserts arrive. I want to announce that Colette and I are engaged to be married!" He bent to kiss the exuberant Colette as everyone gasped. Then the girlfriends all clapped and cheered. Roman, who used his words sparingly, tapped his spoon on the side of a goblet in applause.

Azalea did not miss the wink Philippe directed at his brother. Yet beside her, Sebastian raised a goblet and said, "*À la nôtre!* To a good life!"

All echoed the toast and drank.

Colette extended her hand to reveal an acorn-sized diamond ring. "I didn't slip it on until just now," she said. "We wanted to surprise everyone."

"It's lovely," Cecile cooed. Philippe's mother walked around to hug the couple and congratulate them.

And Azalea noticed Roman's expression as

he quietly observed. There was not so much a proud smile on the father's face as a curious moue. He cast his glance between both of the sons he'd pitted against one another. Was he reveling in the competition? One had already achieved half success. Or was he plotting something else? It bothered her in a way she couldn't quite label.

And then she realized how this must make Sebastian feel. She slid her hand under the table and clasped his hand. A good squeeze brought his attention to her and she kissed him. "He hasn't won yet," she said.

"Doesn't matter," he murmured. "It…really doesn't. What matters is the way you look at me."

With that, Sebastian stood and made another toast to the couple's future and the entire family.

Once desserts were served it was Roman's turn for a speech. He stood and thanked them all for their support. According to Sebastian's whispers in her ear as he translated for his father. The family had been speaking both French and English through the night, but Azalea would not expect the patriarch to employ English when he already had difficulty with speech.

"Family means more now than ever," Sebastian translated. "He is happy."

Dear old Dad having a change of heart about

family? Interesting? And she hoped, for Sebastian's sake, it would develop into gentler, less aggressive expectations of his sons. But still she felt uncomfortable about the whole thing. Something was brewing inside Roman Mercier's brain.

After desserts were cleared and the champagne was poured with elan by the sommelier, everyone chatted quietly. Philippe was showing off his fiancée's ring to his dad and Cecile, explaining how it cost two million but he'd got it for half that thanks to his connections in the jewelry industry.

"Sebastian," Angelique said over a sip of champagne, "you look so well. I don't think I've seen you since Roman was in the hospital. What is it that's got your eyes so bright, my love?"

"Well, isn't it obvious? Zee here is the one who makes me happy."

Eyeing Azalea over her goblet, Angelique made a dismissive noise. Red nails rapped the crystal. "Interesting. Not your usual type."

"Mother," Sebastian admonished.

She shrugged and Azalea felt that the woman would not be dissuaded from what felt like a venture into villainy. Likely she'd been waiting for just the moment to toss out a few comments.

"She's rather unkempt," Angelique said. "And so thick around the middle."

"Mother!" Sebastian remanded with a pound

of his fist on the table that alerted everyone to hesitate in their conversations. "That thick middle is a baby."

Everyone at the table turned their full attention to Azalea.

Sebastian, not seeming to notice he'd silenced the room, continued, "*My* baby, Mother."

Now gasps swept up like a violent wave that crashed against Azalea's skin and flooded into her heart. Philippe swore. Roman tilted his head, and then nodded in what looked like approval. Elaine cooed, saying "*Ooh, la, la!* Another Mercier baby!"

The heat that rose in Azalea's throat to circle her neck felt suffocating. Why had he announced that? They'd agreed not to tell anyone tonight. When she felt him reach for her hand she tugged away and stood. "Excuse me. I need some air."

She fled the table, leaving surprised gasps, remarks that she was rather touchy, and someone congratulating Sebastian on having secured one half of his success.

CHAPTER FIFTEEN

AZALEA MADE A beeline for the ladies' room. Thankful no one was inside, she aimed for the last of the three sinks and leaned over it. She wanted to splash water on her face but thought better against ruining her makeup. The oval mirror showed no black mascara smears from the few teardrops that had escaped as she'd rushed away from the dining room.

What Sebastian's mother had said about her had been cruel.

But Sebastian announcing to all, in a boasting manner, that she carried his child, had gone beyond. How dare he? It hadn't been his place. They had agreed not to tell anyone tonight. This was her body, her baby. And if Sebastian thought to use it as a means to gain control of L'Homme Mercier, he had another think coming.

It had to have been a slip of the tongue. He wouldn't throw her under the bus like that. Or maybe he'd simply needed to feel some pride at that moment? Some small win after Philippe's engagement announcement.

Wrapping her arms across her chest she paced. She studied her stomach in the mirrors as she passed before them. Thick in the middle? Why couldn't she have a baby bump instead of this full-middle swelling? It did look like she'd gone a little too hard on the sweets and carbs. Maybe she had been enjoying Diane's home-made crumpets a little too much lately. With blueberry jam. And lots of butter.

Azalea Grace was definitely not one of those glamorous women sitting out at the table. As nipped, tucked and contoured as they were. Not…sophisticated. So how had she even caught Sebastian's eye in the first place?

Right. She'd taken him by surprise by commandeering the back of his limo. And then they'd spent the best night together. And since, whenever they were together, she really thought they enjoyed one another's company. Had amazing chemistry. She was happy that if she were to have a child, half its genes would be from the smart, sexy, adorable and terribly funny Sebastian Mercier.

But if she had to raise that child within the family sitting out in the dining room?

She shook her head.

The door opened. Azalea turned to the vanity and made it look as though she were checking her hair. Angelique sidled up alongside her, sequins hissing with her movements, and studied her reflection in the adjacent mirror before speaking.

"Sebastian says I must apologize for calling you thick. Apparently, truth is not always welcome. I am sorry."

What an apology. So genuine. Not.

"You are unlike any of my son's previous girlfriends," she said to Azalea's reflection. "They were all very stylish and…"

"I'm sorry, Angelique. I don't meet the standards you have set for your son. I know the Mercier family is rich and has style and a certain social standing. It's not my world, and it never will be. But his abrupt announcement about the baby—"

"Ah, that is the bright side to this startling evening, *oui*?"

Azalea turned to face the woman who granted her a bright smile quite opposite of the treatment she'd just served her.

"You are going to have my son's baby! He is already halfway to the CEO position. You've only to marry him and he wins."

Azalea's mouth dropped open. Tears again threatened, but she held them back with an act of willpower. The woman was truly lacking in empathy.

"I would have chosen a different mate for him," Angelique continued, unaware of her stinging words, "but it gets him what he deserves, so I will go along with it."

Go along with it? As if the woman had any say over any of this!

"You will marry him?"

"He hasn't asked." Why had she said that? It didn't matter! She wasn't going to insert herself further in this messy family drama. "Besides, I wouldn't marry your son. And he knows that."

Angelique's expression remained the same. Because everything on her face was unnaturally tightened. But Azalea suspected she would frown, if she could.

"Just because I'm carrying Sebastian's baby doesn't mean he gets to jump in and assume control. I have choices. And I'm not going to marry a man just to help him win some stupid family competition. It's so cruel that his father subjects him to such a thing!"

"You mustn't speak of Roman like that. He simply demands the best from his sons. His expectations are exactly the reason why Sebastian and Philippe have done so well. They are highly respected by their peers in the industry. Both are millionaires. And how dare you suggest you will keep my son from his child's life!"

No, she could never do that, but— Walking into this crazy argument had not been on the books for tonight. The past few months Azalea had felt emotionally fragile, and as if she were walking uncharted grounds. And speaking with Sebastian's mom only lifted that fragility to the surface. She couldn't hold it together much longer.

"I don't want to argue with you about something that should be between me and Sebastian."

Angelique grabbed her by the arm. "Sebastian is my son. And..." Was that an attempt at a frown? "I don't want him to be like his father."

Her desperate confession startled Azalea. Had the woman empathy after all? Of course, who would want their child to be a man who collected women and sons as if prizes? And now that she thought about it, she realized Sebastian was doing just that! He had emulated his father's example. He'd offered to pay her expenses for a lifetime. Just as Roman had done for his sons' mothers. And she had accepted!

What a fool she had been to allow herself to get sucked into the Mercier family drama.

"I know that as his mother, you think very highly of your son," Azalea started, "as you should. He's amazing. Talented, smart, kind and so funny. We seem to get one another despite our differences. But I could never marry him, even if he did ask. If it was simply to win a competition, then it could never be real. I don't want to live like that."

"Has Sebastian told you he loves you?"

"Well…he has." At least, he'd said he was falling for her. "But…"

"But what? If you know my son as you think you do, you know he does not lie."

No, he did not. Azalea couldn't imagine a lie coming from Sebastian's mouth.

"So, if he has told you he loves you, why do you believe that is a lie?" Angelique challenged.

Because there were too many other conditions distorting that truth. And maybe she just needed to step back from this crazy family to see it all clearly.

"I know he wouldn't lie to me," Azalea replied. "And I do believe I love him. But it feels wrong. This. Your family. It's…crushing in on me. I'm sorry."

With that, Azalea fled the bathroom, but waiting outside across the hall from the door stood Sebastian, hands in his pockets. He straightened, pleading with his soft yet devastating gaze.

Azalea put up her hand. "I don't want to do this. Not here. I'm going home." Dash it, she couldn't flee. Home to her right now was Sebastian's place. "I just need to get away from this drama."

"I'll text the driver to pick you up and take you back to my place," he offered.

"Thank you." When he made to take her hand, she shook her head. "I need some space, Sebastian."

Angelique strolled out of the ladies' room and took her son's arm. "I tried," she said to him. "She's not got the Mercier dedication to family."

"Mother, enough. You were only to apologize to Zee."

"She did," Azalea said. "And there are some things your mother and I agree on."

Angelique lifted her chin proudly.

But there had been no agreement on the definition of family.

"You are a good man," Azalea said to him. "I have never believed otherwise." She wandered toward the elevator. "I'll talk to you later. Please, just give me an hour or so to myself."

"I can do that. I'm sorry, Zee!" he called as she stepped onto the elevator.

Before the doors closed, she saw Sebastian with his mother standing beside him, clutching his arm like the protective yet unknowingly wicked mother who could never unfurl her tentacles from around her child. Azalea felt terrible leaving in such a manner. It didn't reflect well on Sebastian. And she didn't want to hurt him.

But this was all too much to process.

The man had once offered to defend her honor. What had happened to his valiant promise? Did his family stifle that individuality, his genuine impulse to do right? It seemed like it. They loved him but they wanted certain things from him, and he had unknowingly fallen right in line.

CHAPTER SIXTEEN

BEFORE SEBASTIAN ENTERED his home, he leaned against the wall and took the ring box out from inside his suit coat. It had been nestled there all night. He opened the velvet box. Inside sat a 10 carat diamond ring surrounded by sapphires as pale as Zee's eyes. It wasn't the same ring he'd utilized two times previously. He'd returned that and purchased one that was fitting of Zee's beauty, her soft innocence and her bubbly nature. He'd intended to propose to her after a successful family dinner.

Now? He'd blown it. Everything felt wrong.

His mother could be cruel in her forthright manner. Angelique was a judgmental person but also honest. Yet he hadn't expected her to treat Zee with such open disdain. He should have never allowed her to go into the ladies' room to apologize. After they'd watched Zee's exit, she'd told him Zee had threatened to take the baby and never allow him to see it.

He couldn't know if that was true or an exaggeration. He suspected the latter. It was Angelique's habit. What was it that she and Zee could have possibly agreed on? He should have asked his mother, but he'd wanted to get away from her as much as Zee had. They had returned to the dining room. He'd hugged Colette and Philippe, congratulating them both. To Sebastian's surprise, their engagement didn't bother him at all. He didn't feel as though he'd slipped in the race to the prize. And yet…

Tucking away the ring box, he blew out a breath. He should have never blurted to all that Zee was pregnant. In that moment he had felt pride and exhilaration to make such an announcement. But at the sight of Zee's sad expression, he'd immediately known he'd done wrong. He should have asked her permission to make the announcement. And…when he was really honest with himself, the first set of eyes he'd met after breaking the news had been Philippe's. His brother's gape had pleased him. He'd successfully created an heir! Halfway to the prize. He and Philippe were still on equal ground.

He swore and caught the heel of his palm against the doorframe. Was he so callous as to use Azalea in such a manner? To gain the CEO position? The baby hadn't been planned.

It wasn't as though he had plotted his way to the win. But any proposal of marriage now could only be seen by Azalea as his final step to securing that position.

And maybe it was.

That his father had patted him on the back and told him, "Good job," had again bolstered his pride. For a few moments. And then he'd surfaced from that false emotion and realized that Azalea didn't see any of this in the way his family did.

Or maybe she saw it for exactly what it was.

He was following in Roman Mercier's footsteps. Because if he did propose, Zee would surely run away from him. And that left him only with the option of providing for her, financially taking care of his family. Just as his father did for his sons and girlfriends. Sebastian hadn't even seen it coming. It had obviously been ingrained in him all his life. But that was no excuse. It couldn't be.

Damn this stupid competition!

There was no way to erase the damage it had inflicted on his and Azalea's relationship. And they did have a relationship. He cared deeply about her. He loved her.

Or was he telling himself he loved her because it felt like what was expected? He couldn't know if it was because his heart hadn't taken the full jump or rather if it was all this family stuff that was deflecting any real emotion from fully forming.

Again, damn it all!

He knew this was difficult for Zee. And that she was pregnant on top of all this had to compound her stress. But it was hard for him, too. He didn't want to mess this up. But he wasn't sure how to make it right. And…what was right?

Inside his home it was dark save for ambient city lights beaming through the wall of windows. Was she already asleep? She needed to rest for the baby.

He tiptoed through the house, leaving his suit coat on the back of the sofa and taking his shoes off before slinking into the bedroom. The lamp by the bed was on and Zee stood beside it in the red silk negligee he'd bought for her.

"Hey," she said.

"Did I wake you?"

"Nope. Can't sleep."

"I'm sorry. I wanted to give you some time."

"Thank you for that." She sat on the bed and patted it beside her thigh. "Let's talk."

He noticed her pallor. "Are you feeling okay?"

"My tummy was a little unsettled after dinner. Might have been that taste of octopus."

"Or the judgmental mother?"

She smiled and clasped his hand, tilting her

head onto his shoulder. "Angelique is an interesting one. But she's your mother. And I can see that you both love one another. I don't want to do anything to change that between the two of you."

"You wouldn't and you haven't. Angelique can be abrupt and has a tendency to speak her mind. She wants the best for me."

"I know that. And I realize that, no matter what happens between the two of us, those people I met tonight are forever going to be my baby's aunts, uncles and grandparents."

"Henri and Charles will have a niece or nephew close to their age with whom they can play."

"It was nice to see you interacting with Henri. You really like the little guy, don't you?"

"He's my brother. And he's silly. Loves when you blow on his toes. You should hear his giggles. Charles, on the other hand, is a sober bit of pudge and baby goo."

"The fact that you notice such defining traits in them makes me believe you would make the best dad, Sebastian."

"You think so? Better than Roman?"

"Well, I don't know your dad at all. And I shouldn't judge him on the one quality alone. But he does seem to want to pit his sons against one another for reasons that are—" She sighed. "I just can't see you doing something like that to your children."

"I would never." And yet…here he was. Committing much the same crime against the family structure as his father had.

"And your mother…well, Sebastian, she's quite dependent on your father, isn't she?"

"He does finance her entire existence." As he had offered to do for Zee? *Mon Dieu*, why had he not seen that one for what it was?

"And is that how you wish me to be? You offered to pay for things, and—I shouldn't have accepted. I'll give back all of it."

"Don't do that, Zee. I don't want you to be dependent on me. You won't be. You'll get established with the baby and then find a job that suits you so you can feel as though you are making your own way."

She frowned.

"Or not?" he added with a shrug. He didn't know how to read her mood. Whatever he said would be wrong, no matter if it sounded right to him.

"I won't become another kept woman like those girlfriends who sat around the table tonight."

And he didn't want that for her, but his offer would do just that. How to allow her the freedom she obviously desired but also provide her the help he knew she required to survive?

"Despite it all," she said, "your mother loves

you and she only wants the best for you and your family."

"Is that so terrible?"

"It isn't."

"As for my dad, I sometimes think the competition and race for the top is all he knows. His father was the same. Roman was one of four boys who eventually won ownership of L'Homme Mercier after much the same sort of competition. Except my dad had to produce an heir *without* marrying. My grandfather didn't want the woman involved in the family wealth. Which is why he's never married."

"That explains some things. Yet I wonder why he's insisted now his sons marry?"

"Might have something to do with his brush with mortality. The first stroke is what served as catalyst to this competition. On the other hand, Dad is always energized to watch Philippe and me compete."

"So odd. But again, I shouldn't judge. Sounds like the only lifestyle he's ever known. I find it interesting that he still keeps all his sons' mothers in his life."

"Kind of crazy, eh? Roman does love family. In his manner. And if he had refused my mother to be a part of my life, I may have hated him for that."

"I suppose. You are not a playboy like your father."

"A man can't work in the fashion industry, surrounded by beautiful women, and not have his roguish moments." He clasped her hand and kissed the back of it. "Not anymore. I honestly have no desire to date any other woman, Zee. And it's not even about the fact you're carrying my child. I care about you. I want you in my life."

"I want the same."

"You do?" He searched her gaze, smiling a little. "Then why are we at this crossroads that feels as though one of us is going to turn in the opposite direction and leave the other standing alone?"

"You know how I feel about us marrying."

"Fake. Which it wouldn't be, Zee. Not to me."

"That's where your mother and I agree. We both know you are true to your word. When you tell me you feel as though you are falling in love with me, I know you are speaking from the heart."

"I am. And I promise you nothing about a marriage between us would be fake."

A kiss was necessary to his wanting heart. Their connection did not cease to make his world feel right. Even if in reality it was not right. He caressed her hair and she sank into their kiss.

He didn't want to lose her. He didn't know how to keep her. He'd never been more at odds in his life.

"My father has made this difficult," he said when he pulled away. "I don't want to blame him. It's all on me. Where I'm standing right now. The situation life has presented to me." He stroked her cheek and she leaned against his hand. Her quiet acceptance both filled his heart and broke it at the same time. "I don't know how I could have made a different choice, Zee. You did hijack me."

She smirked. "Guilty. But you did invite me to the party, and your bed."

"You could have refused."

"I couldn't have possibly refused the sexy Frenchman who danced into my heart."

"Would you stay with me if I asked?"

"Here in Paris?"

He nodded.

"That's just it. I don't know. I can use the excuse that Paris is another big city that makes me feel uncomfortable, but the thing is, I feel comfortable wherever I am as long as you're holding my hand."

He pressed her hand to his lips. Losing her felt inevitable. Because at the moment, this—whatever it was they had—felt more forced than right. As if they were both avoiding speaking the truth. But he didn't know his truth. *Did* he love her? He'd been speaking the word, but had he a grasp on its true meaning? How to know what love really was when all his life it had been expressed through expectations, challenges, boasts and achievements?

"I love you, Sebastian."

His heart thudded and then dropped. It felt too tremendous and too small at the same time. Because if he replied in kind he wasn't sure if it would be accepted in kind.

"But I don't think we can make this work," she said. "Not the way your family wants it to look."

Now his heart dropped to his gut. A swallow tasted of acrid heartache.

"Can you tell me it can work?" she challenged.

"I don't know what you want to hear, Zee. Rather, I do. I know what your heart craves from me. But…right now? I feel like I'll break your heart no matter what move I make. And I don't want to be like Roman. I can't be. Someone has to break the cycle."

"I'm proud of you for recognizing that."

He closed his eyes. Yes, and he'd only just made such a realization this evening.

He hadn't swept Zee off her feet and given her good reason to surrender to a future with him in it. Because that ring box in his pocket out in the living room was not the thing to make it all better. He needed to win her heart, soul and trust.

If he'd ever had her in the first place.

"I'm returning to Grace Farm tomorrow," she said. "I think it's best. I need to spend time on the farm before it's sold and gone forever. It holds a lot of memories for me."

"I don't want you to leave me, but I understand. Of course, you'll need to send off Stella and Daisy."

They sat in silence for what seemed a lifetime, though he suspected it was only a few minutes. Zee laid her head on his shoulder and snuggled against his arm. How was it possible she could smell like summer when the moment felt like winter? Was this the end? Were they breaking it off forever? He didn't want that. But he didn't know how to ask for forever from her.

"We've come to a certain agreement about the baby," she said. "I will accept the financial help you've offered. If it's still on the table."

"Of course, it is. I would never rescind that offer."

"Thank you. Sebastian. But I won't take your money forever. I promise I'll figure my life out and get a good job sooner rather than later. I'll be able to support myself. And eventually I won't need your assistance. Because it feels like we'd be perpetuating your dad's..."

Yes, his father's ways. And his father before him. What a legacy the Mercier family flaunted.

"There are some aspects of what we have that feel different than Roman and his girlfriends. It does to me. I mean, the emotional part of it all. With hope, you'll realize that as well. I will never stop supporting you, Zee."

"I..." She sniffled and tears rolled down her cheeks.

That she hurt so deeply tore apart his bewildered heart. He felt that sadness as much as she did, but he didn't know how to express it. So he settled for ignoring the shards of his heart that seemed to crackle and fall.

He pulled Zee into a hug and kissed the top of her soft, sweet-smelling hair. "Things will go as they should," he said.

It was more of an encouragement to his own heart. It was all he could manage without crying himself.

She would leave him. Take his baby with her. And he might never see her again.

No. He wouldn't allow that. And not because he was some rich bastard who could have anything he wanted with the wave of his wallet. No, he wanted Azalea in his life—baby or not. And there may yet be a way to win her.

"Will you go with me somewhere tomorrow morning?" he asked. "It's someplace I want you to see before you leave. I'll put you on a private jet back to England after."

"What is it?"

"Just something I want you to see. I promise there will be no Mercier family members there."

She nuzzled her head onto his shoulder. "Sure. One last trip together, then."

Such a final announcement. Now Sebastian had to tilt back his head to staunch the tears from falling. He was so close to losing her.

CHAPTER SEVENTEEN

AZALEA HAD NO idea what to expect when Sebastian pulled around the front of the building in a blue sports car. He'd told her he kept it for summer driving and hadn't yet had it out this year. Now they cruised out of Paris to a destination he said was an hour's drive away.

Anything to spend a little more time with him before she left for home. Because while she knew going back to the farm was best for her, she hated that decision in equal measure. Leaving the one man she loved couldn't be right. Was it pregnancy hormones screwing with her mental reasoning? Possibly.

Her life had suddenly become so big. She was swimming in new experiences and yet grasping for something solid and familiar. It was hard to process the entirety of it all. So she decided to take it one day at a time. And do it with pastries. Sebastian had kindly pulled over in front of a patisserie and she'd bought croissants and chocolate-stuffed rolls. But when he'd given her the side-eye as she started to pull one out of the bag, she'd said she'd wait until they stopped. Didn't want crumbs on the leather upholstery.

Now he drove down a quiet country road lined with thick emerald grass that wavered in the breeze. Tall birch and lush maple blocked the sunlight for a second, then a dash of warmth hit her nose again. Rolling down the window filled the car with fresh air.

"You know that Pierre Hermé in Paris delivers pastries on subscription?" he said as he pulled into a driveway before a medium-sized, stone-faced château.

"Really? I wonder if they'd deliver to England?"

"I can look into it."

The offer was too rich to accept, but on the other hand, when pregnancy cravings nudged… "Go for it."

With a kiss to her cheek, he leaned over and opened her door for her. "I appreciate that you don't argue the simple things, Zee."

"When life offers me a party, I party. And when it offers pastries, I am no fool. Where are we?" she asked as he swung around the back of the car and met her as she stepped from the car.

Before them rose a château that could almost claim quaint cottage-ness for its size, were it not for the tall windows on the two floors and so much slate tile on the roof. The yard hugging the gravel drive was overgrown, the grass as high as their knees. Oak trees dipped their boughs over the front doorway where pink flowers bloomed and designed an elaborate trellis.

"Oh my gosh!" Azalea rushed toward the frothy pink blooms. "Do you know what these are?"

Sebastian shrugged. "Flowers?"

She plucked a bloom and tucked it in her hair, spinning to declare, "These are azaleas!"

"Really? Then this adventure was meant to be."

"Whose place is this?"

He shuffled in his pocket for a ring of keys. "It used to belong to my grandparents on my mother's side. When they passed away, the property went to me. I haven't been out here since I was a kid who got dumped with Grand-père and Grand-mère every summer while Mom and Roman took a vacation overseas. Or Mom and whomever she was dating at the time. Though I did stop in a few years ago when it came to me. A grounds crew and cleaning service stop in twice a year. Let's go inside."

The house was cool and bright enough to navigate without switching on the lights. The electricity was kept shut off, he explained, as well as the water. Sturdy white canvas dust covers hugged the furniture in the front sitting room. In the kitchen, counters were also covered and glass-faced cupboards were bare. The place had been cleared of the smaller things and decorations, leaving behind only large furniture and appliances. He led her toward the back of the main sitting area, which opened to a stone patio overgrown with weeds.

"It needs some love," he said as he walked out onto the grass and weed-frothed stones. "Maybe a cow or some chickens?"

"Are you asking me or telling me?"

The air smelled so good that Azalea felt compelled to spin, eyes closed and head tilted back. This felt like her dad's farm. Safe and cozy. And the sun beaming on her cheeks made her forget about last night's debacle.

"I'm asking."

Suddenly he twirled her and they did a little dance. It was always easy to find their silent rhythm. Kicking off her shoes, she shimmied her hips and plugged her nose, performing the dance move that he mirrored. Then with a grand flair, he spun her under his arm and performed their patented dip that activated her libido every single time. When she rose in his embrace, he kissed her deeply.

Kissing Sebastian always felt right. Like something she deserved. They knew one another in an intimate, silent way that said more than words could ever begin to define. Safety in his embrace. And excitement. An exhilaration of discovery and a confidence of ease. There was no one else in this world she'd rather be kissing. And she could kiss him for the rest of their lives.

That thought made her pull back.

"Why did we come here?" she asked. "Did you want me to see where you were most happy as a child?"

"That and… I want you to have it, Zee."

"Have what?"

"This place." He dangled the keys before her. "The property. It would be perfect to raise a little boy, yes?"

"Well, yes, but…"

"You like a farm, but you still prefer to be close to a city," he pointed out. "I know it would mean you'd have to move to France, but…will you accept? I promise it's not like I'm tucking you away out here to keep you for myself."

Now that he brought it up… "That's exactly what it sounds like, Sebastian."

"I…" He exhaled heavily. "I wrestled on the drive here with the whole 'tucking away the girlfriend and her child' scenario. It might look like it, but it doesn't feel that way in my heart. I'm not Roman Mercier. At least, I hope that I will not follow in that most egregious of his traits. I so desperately want to be different, Zee."

She could see that in him. She wanted it to be that way if that was what he truly desired. But could he rise from his conditioned ways to forge a new path?

"I want you to have this place to do with as you will," he said. "A place that will make you feel safe. But also, I want to be close so I can visit my son. You will allow me to do that?"

"Of course, I wouldn't forbid you from being a part of our child's life. But. This is a very generous offer, Sebastian. This home holds memories for you. How can you give it away?"

"Maybe I want to put new memories here to share with the old ones? And as I've said, I haven't used it since it came to me. It would be a shame for it to sit empty when there's a bright soul who could bring happiness to its walls and grounds."

"It's a lot to take in. I mean, it's beautiful. And it would require a lot of work..."

Which would keep her busy. And she'd start with this patio, plucking out the weeds and maybe planting some rosemary along the borders for fragrance. And wouldn't a birdbath painted in bright colors be a lovely addition?

"The grounds and cleaning crews can come

in this week and polish it up for you," he said. "You can select a decorator to do up the inside. Or do what you like by yourself. It's completely up to you."

Oh, baby, what fun she could have making the place her own. Could it ever be her own coming from a man who struggled with doing the right thing and who may eventually revert to his father's ways? Then, the place may become like a cage to her and her child. Oh!

"I have to think about this."

"Of course, you do. You only jump into things when the door is open and you're being chased."

She smirked at his reference to their first night together. That was the night her heart knew Sebastian was the man for her. Yes, even when her brain continued to insist he was not.

"Here." He took her hand and placed the key ring on her palm. "Take these with you. I'll text you the GPS coordinates for the property. You can come here whenever you like. Move in. Do what you wish. But please accept this from me, Zee?"

"I..." She dangled the key ring from her fingers, thinking how much fun it would be to decorate the place and make it her own.

To make a life for her new family.

It was too generous. But that was simply Sebastian doing what made him happy. And what a perfect place to raise her child. "…will take these keys and give it a good think. How does that sound?"

"I can't ask for anything more. Well, I could, but I don't want to push you into anything. Now, let's get you to England."

"You want to be rid of me so quickly?"

"No, I want you to stay with me." He slid his hands down her arms. His touch always served her a good shiver. Was it her heart responding to his heart? Nah, it was base and wanting, completely lustful. "But I also want you to do things your way, in your time. And I did arrange for the pilot to meet us at the airport in about an hour and half."

"Then let's get going."

Azalea locked the door and clutched the keys to her breast the entire ride to the airport. It felt like she held her future in her hands. And within her body. Yet beside her sat a piece to that puzzle that didn't seem to orient itself to fall neatly into place.

CHAPTER EIGHTEEN

Weeks later

STELLA AND DAISY, carefully loaded on a livestock trailer, rolled down the driveway and away from Grace Farm. Azalea waved, and—dash it—sniffed back a few tears. It was silly to get so attached to a farm animal.

"Hormones," she muttered. That was her story, and she was sticking to it.

Oliver Grace returned from the front gate, having pounded the Sold sign into the ground earlier this morning. They had two weeks to vacate the premises. Both her dad and Diane were ready to go, with most of their possessions packed. They weren't taking any large furniture. Only clothing and necessities. Because they intended to travel the world for a few years before—if even—settling somewhere.

"Where do you think you'll ultimately land?" Azalea asked as her dad wrapped an arm across her shoulders and they stood before the cottage watching the trailer disappear down the road.

"England will always be my home. I'm not sure I could ever leave it completely. Diane thinks Greece."

"Beautiful water and the sun." She tilted her head against her dad's. "Sounds like a dreamy place to stay for a while."

"How you feeling, Lea?"

"Great, actually." She smoothed a palm over her belly. "Finally this extra weight is turning into some semblance of a baby bump so I don't just look fat."

He laughed. "Your mother was the same way with both you and Dahlia. When are you due?"

"February."

"Then we'll plan to be in France after the New Year."

Yes, France. Because she'd spent the last few weeks muddling, creating scenarios, mentally arguing, and then finally deciding that, yes, she would move to the château south of Paris. She would be a fool not to accept such a generous offer, especially since her desire to go job hunting never seemed to match her need to take it easy. To honor her changing body and heart.

Besides, this farm was no longer her home. And she couldn't be a rural princess in a low-rent London flat.

She looked forward to the adventure of it all. And while she could never know if Sebastian would be a common fixture or an infrequent visitor, she had talked herself into accepting whatever he decided would work best for him.

Did she want him to live with her? To help her raise their child? Yes. And…she knew she could do this on her own, if need be, but…yes.

"You going to be all right, sweetie?"

"I am. Off to adventure! And with Dahlia helping me move in, I think I'll have a great start."

Her sister had vacation time and planned to stay with Azalea for a couple of weeks. Painting, weeding, decorating and lots of gossip, was how she'd put it. And shopping for baby things.

Her dad kissed her cheek and then mentioned Diane would have supper ready soon.

It had been days since Zee had texted him. Sebastian stood in the office before the window. The sun had set, and the coffee his secretary had brought in earlier was cold. The instant his phone buzzed he spun and picked it up. His heart fluttered to see a text from Zee.

I'm at the château. Here to stay. My sister is helping me move in and make it a home. Wanted you to know I think of you every day. Want to see you. But give me some time?

She'd accepted his offer to stay at the château. That was immense. He would give her all the time she needed. It wouldn't change the way he felt about her. Now more than ever he had to win her heart. Because being CEO of the company wouldn't matter if he didn't have Azalea Grace in his life.

"That turned out much better than I thought it would," Dahlia said of the bedroom wall that they had dry-brushed with shades of maroon, violet and pink. "Gives it some warmth in a rustic kind of way. Not my style, but I think it's you, Lea."

"I love it." Azalea tilted her bottled water against Dahlia's wineglass. "Thanks for helping me with everything these past few weeks. The baby's room is adorable."

They'd found simple pine furnishings for the small room next to the main bedroom. It was a sunny room with a balcony, so Azalea could sit in the rocker on warm summer nights.

"I'm excited about this," she said with a smooth over her belly. "I feel like this little guy is eagerly waiting to come into my life."

The doctor had accidentally revealed the baby's sex after a sonogram and Sebastian had been right. A boy. Azalea hadn't cared whether it was a boy or girl. She was simply ready to hold the little tyke and mom the heck out of it.

"You do have that proverbial glow, sis. You know I'm not the motherly sort, but you almost make me want to have one, too."

"Do you think Clyve would make a good dad?"

Dahlia's boyfriend had proposed last year but they hadn't set a date. They were in no rush, both working in the legal sector and having eighty-hour workweeks. Who had time to say vows?

"Maybe. I don't know. It wouldn't be fair to a kid with our work schedules. That's what I love about your situation. Your man is taking care of everything so all you have to do is be a mom. How perfect is that?"

It could be more perfect. Like having that man in her life to actually be a father to her son. Not being relegated to the cottage where she had her own life and he had his in the city. She tried not to overthink it. Sebastian had gifted her the world with his generosity. And if that meant she'd be just another girlfriend sitting around the monthly family dinner, she had to accept that.

But did she really?

"You're thinking about it again," Dahlia warned. "I shouldn't have brought him up. You always go all melancholy on me when I do."

"I love him, Dahlia. This château is a dream, but it's not the perfect dream."

"You need the father in the picture rather than floating around the edges."

"Exactly."

"Do you think Sebastian would make a good father?"

"I actually do. The little I've seen him interact with his baby brothers makes me believe he would be a kind and gentle dad. But then, what do we ever know about how well we can parent before we've even given it a go? I just hope I can be the best mother and raise a boy who is respectful and kind."

"You will. And if his dad does more than float around the edges that would be ideal. Maybe you should ask him to marry you."

"Can I do that?"

"Heck, yeah. But I get the struggle you have over that stupid family competition debacle. You'd never know if he married you for love or money."

"His brother is engaged right now. There's always a chance Philippe could win. But I really want Sebastian to win. Oh, why am I being like this? I can help him to win something he wants more than anything."

"At what price? Your heart? Your trust for him? Standing in line next to the other girlfriends? I can't see you getting a boob job."

Azalea sighed and settled onto the floor before the bed. The fake fur rug was soft and dark pink to match one of the colors on the wall. "Tell me what to do, Dahlia."

"I think you're doing it." Her sister sat next to her. They each slanted a foot toward one another, touching toes as they'd always done when they were kids. "You're capable of doing the single mom thing. It'll be much easier with financial help than not. And you've got a dream home. What more is there?"

"A dream man."

Dahlia sighed dramatically. "Give me the bloke's address. I'll stop in to Paris to have a word with him."

"You will not. Sebastian will...*we* will make this work. One way or another."

"Fine. But I'm not going to promise to babysit once the little man arrives."

"I wouldn't expect you to, especially living as far away as you do. But you will have aunt duties."

"What will that involve? I don't think I can bring myself to change a nappy."

"How about throwing a baby shower?"

"Oh, I can do that! Let's go online and shop for baby stuff!"

When, within five minutes of introducing himself to Oliver Grace, the man asked Sebastian to help him out back, he agreed eagerly. A means to ingratiate himself to Zee's dad? And to get to know him better. He'd flown over specifically to talk to the man. What better way than to do it within Oliver's comfort zone?

Apparently, comfort meant mud and hay. Donning the rubber boots once again, Sebastian helped Oliver heft a dozen bales of hay that had been dropped off by a neighboring farmer to store in the overhead loft of the barn. They were heavy but not overly taxing. After a few bales he got into the swing of it, and it felt good to work up a sweat. Even wearing a dress shirt and trousers.

When they had finished and Oliver invited him to stand at the back of the barn where it opened to the fenced field, which was absent any cows, Sebastian had to ask. "Where are Stella and her baby?"

"Sold them."

Right. Zee had mentioned something about her dad selling them. She had been heartbroken. He'd seen it in her expression. A woman and her cow were not so easily separated by the heartstrings.

"Then why the hay?"

Oliver shrugged. "I bought those bales this spring. Forgot about them. They'll be good starter stock for the new owners."

"When do you move?"

"Few days. We're headed to the States for six months. Diane wants to tour all fifty states. Not sure we can do it all in that time, but we'll give it a go."

"Why the time limit? If your intent is to travel, then why set a schedule?"

"Exactly." He smirked. "But she's the one with the schedule in her head. You must know how schedules work. Big-city businessman like you."

"I do, but I've learned to be more lenient thanks to your daughter."

Oliver nodded, but Sebastian noticed his tight jaw. He could guess what the man must think of him. So he'd end the torture.

"I had to talk to you face-to-face," Sebastian said, "because your daughter is important to me. I love her." He waited for Oliver's reaction, but the man merely inclined his head. Listening.

Yes, he did love Zee. He'd created his definition of the word, and it felt right in his heart. It was that immense feeling he got every time he saw her blue eyes crinkle and her freckles dance. The feeling that all things were right.

"I know she'll be the best mother."

"Yes, she will. But what about the father? What does he intend to do?"

"That's why I'm here. Monsieur Grace, I want to ask you for your daughter's hand in marriage. I love her. But I don't want to ask her to marry me without your permission."

Oliver stood from his lean against the barn wall, crossing his arms over his chest. Defensive? Not a good sign.

"I'm sure she's told you about the competition with my brother."

Oliver nodded. Swatted at a fly.

"It's why I haven't felt right about asking her to marry me. But I intend to tell my dad I'm out. I love Zee too much to risk losing her. And if that means I have to step out of the competition, then I will."

"Won't marrying my daughter make you the winner?"

Sebastian exhaled heavily. "It would. But it wouldn't be right. Not to Zee. I know she would always wonder if I asked her to marry her out of love, or if it was to win a competition. I can't do that to her. It must be real with her. The one thing we value most between us is truth."

"Noble. But..."

Sebastian met the man's gaze. Same pale blue as Zee's eyes. But not so fun-loving and perhaps even cynical right now.

"Lea's told me that winning that CEO position would make you a happy man."

Sebastian nodded. "It would. I believe L'Homme Mercier should remain true to its legacy by continuing its attention to menswear, but my brother has different plans. Much as I hate to see the company add a women's department under Philippe's control, stepping out of the competition is a sacrifice I am willing to make."

"Not for my daughter you won't."

"I…don't understand."

"I don't give you permission to marry my daughter."

"But—"

Oliver held up a hand. "I understand that you love Lea. It fills my heart to know my grandchild has a father who will love him and his mother. Even if he isn't in their life."

"But I want to be—"

"You asked for my permission? Well, you've got your answer. I won't have you marrying my daughter if it means sacrificing something that would make you happy. It wouldn't be fair to Lea. Happiness is an inside job. That saying about making another person happy is nonsense. Only you can make you happy."

Zee had once said much the same to him. The apple hadn't fallen far from the tree.

"And then?" Oliver continued. "Once you're happy? Then you can find another person who complements that happiness in their special way. But if you think you're doing something noble by walking away from a job you desire to prove your love to Lea? Nope." Oliver shook his head. "Not going to happen."

"I intend to tell my father I'm out of the competition," Sebastian reiterated. "No matter what."

"That's your choice. But if you're serious about my opinion on the future you may have with my daughter? You've heard my say."

Sebastian nodded and bowed his head. The man had a point about making himself happy. But he hated to hear that. That meant he'd have to continue the competition.

He wasn't about to lose Zee, though. There had to be a way to make this right. Which meant, his happiness first, and then he could begin to imagine embracing his family.

Family? Yes, that was the key to all of it. He had to talk to his dad. And he knew what had to go down. Truths must be honored.

"Can I get you a bite to eat before you go?" Oliver offered casually. As if he'd not just torn out Sebastian's heart.

"No, I'm… I just came to ask that one question. I should be on my way."

He started to walk through the barn. What had just gone down? He didn't need Oliver Grace's approval for a single thing. Because that man's approval did not make him feel like a smile from Zee did. Her smile gave him such pride and he felt respected by her, seen. That was all he needed.

And yet, Oliver had a point. Could he truly stand as head of a family if his heart were not made happy by his work? What sort of example would that set for his son? He'd grown up watching his father flit from woman to woman, never committing, and—

It had to stop! It would stop. With him.

"You seem like a good man, Sebastian," Oliver called after him. "I know my daughter loves you."

That small comment landed right in his heart. The Grace family had a way of gifting him respect in a manner he'd never experienced.

Sebastian paused in the open end of the barn and turned back to Oliver. "I'll make it right. I promise."

CHAPTER NINETEEN

DURING THE SHORT flight from London to Paris, Sebastian pulled out his phone. The screensaver was the photo of him clasping Zee around the waist so she wouldn't be carried off by a bouquet of bright balloons. That had been a hell of a night. One that had changed his life.

He opened the video that had been taken moments after that photo. He and Zee had marveled over the display crafted entirely from paper. It had looked like a Japanese cherry tree, spilling blossoms from its slender branches to the ground. They'd stood in the middle of it all, posing for a few photos, and then…their first kiss.

At the time, Sebastian hadn't been aware the photographer had switched his phone to video to record. Afterward, when she'd handed him back the phone she'd apologized, but had said it was a moment she'd thought worthy of capture.

Indeed.

Now he watched as he kissed Zee. They'd both

been exhilarated from dancing and getting to know one another. Like two magnets, they'd instantly clicked. Her freckles had dazzled him. Her bright smile had seeped through his skin and flooded his system with joy. And he realized now he was watching himself as he lost his heart to a woman he had only known for hours. At the time it had felt as if they'd been searching for one another all their lives. Their souls had finally found one another.

A silly thought? No. It had been real. And that beautiful soul now carried his baby. They'd made a new soul together. They belonged together. And not in some weird arrangement where he kept Zee on a farm and visited her on weekends because they weren't married. Or even married because he wanted to gain the CEO position. Their souls wouldn't survive with anything less than true, real connection. No conditions attached.

His heart ached. He'd thought it a noble gesture to fly in and request Oliver Grace for his daughter's hand. He'd never expected a no. But if Sebastian were in Oliver's position, he would have delivered the same answer. And while it wasn't binding, and wouldn't keep Sebastian from doing as he pleased…he would honor that *no*.

Until he could make it right.

* * *

Roman Mercier was recovering slowly but surely following the second stroke. With the use of a cane, his gait touched stability. He'd initially refused the cane, but when Elaine had presented him with a stylish walking stick, he'd ceased argument. It was his voice and his ability to speak fluidly that still troubled him. He could speak but his words were jumbled together and sometimes he chose the wrong word. Aphasia, a condition of the stroke. A speech pathologist worked with him three times a week. Elaine made sure he did not miss the private, in-home sessions. She'd told Sebastian she wanted her twins' father to be able to communicate with them. As well, she'd mentioned her plan to win his father's softening heart by convincing him he should marry the mother of his latest sons.

Sebastian had wished her luck. And he truly hoped she would be successful, if not for his youngest brothers, but for the Mercier family overall. The toxic sins of the father had to be redeemed.

And today Sebastian was taking a step to do just that. There was no time to dally or hope for change. Action must be taken. His future would look different than his father's past.

Sebastian found his dad in the conservatory, which overlooked the narrow garden against the ancient limestone wall that separated their property from the neighbor. Roman was going over some paperwork for L'Homme Mercier. Sebastian realized that even though their patriarch had been felled by the stroke he was still an able and important part of the business. He had connections, a certain trust built up with their oldest and some of their largest clients.

But the man also had two capable sons. It was time he retired or took a smaller role.

Still, Sebastian did not see Philippe as the best choice for CEO. Even if he had no designs on a women's line, the man could be easily distracted by recreational pursuits, which also included women.

"Business on a Saturday?" he asked his dad. He strolled to the window and stood beside his father's lounge chair.

Dressed impeccably, as was his mien, and nursing what looked like whiskey on the rocks in a cut-crystal tumbler—but which smelled more like coffee to Sebastian—his father gestured he sit. He used gestures more frequently as opposed to talking, though Elaine insisted it was important to be patient and allow Roman to speak. That was the only way he was going to improve his speech.

"What are you drinking? Doesn't smell like whiskey."

"Coffee," Roman said with a wince. "Elaine insists…less alcohol."

"Coffee has been touted to have some excellent health benefits. Though cold coffee sounds horrid, if you ask me."

Leaning over to inspect the papers on his father's lap, Sebastian watched as he pulled out a red file folder and handed it to him.

"What is this?"

Roman held up a finger to pause him from opening the file. "Important changes. Life."

"Life?" Curious, but also fearing that Roman had made those changes to the company, Sebastian didn't open the file. "Before we get into this, there's something I came here to tell you. Ask you. Well, both." He sat on the window seat before his father. "I'm in love, *mon père*. With Azalea Grace."

His father nodded. "Your…baby."

"Yes, she's the mother of my child, but that's not why I love her. I fell in love with her months ago. On the first night we met, actually. It just took my brain a while to realize what my heart has known. I know you probably can't understand…"

His father clasped his hand and squeezed. He opened his mouth to speak, so Sebastian waited to allow him to form words. "I…have loved. Do. Love."

"I know. You love your children. You love the mothers of your children. I wasn't implying… Well." To even begin to understand the intricate heart of his father could be a mad-making venture.

"I want to marry Zee," he said. "But not because of some family competition. And yet, if I ask her to marry me, she'll only believe it is because of the competition. And I thought I would come here to tell you I was out. To allow Philippe the win. But I can't do that, either. I genuinely feel I would be the best choice for heading L'Homme Mercier. And certainly, I understand how much you enjoy the work you do with the company, but you must realize it has come time for you to retire, *mon père*. You and Elaine should be spending your hours enjoying the twins."

Now his father leaned forward and slid a palm over the back of Sebastian's hand. They had never been demonstrative in their affection. Winning approval and a congratulatory nod of the old man's head had been the morsels of emotion and fondness Sebastian had learned to accept over the years. So the feel of his father's warm hand on his loosened something inside him. He clasped Roman's hand and bowed his head over it. At a loss for words. He simply wanted to experience this moment. He had almost lost him to a stroke. Twice.

Family did mean something to him. It was everything. And he could have something wondrous if only he'd step up and do it the right way. For perhaps the first time in his life, his heart was telling him which was the right way.

"I don't want to compete with my brother anymore," he said softly. "And I need to change the family dynamic that has existed for generations. It's not what I want. Can you understand?"

His father nodded. He tapped the red folder. "Wrote it. Too much to say. Mean it." He slapped a hand against his heart. "For my sons. Family."

With a heavy sigh, Sebastian opened the folder. He'd not clearly explained what he needed to his father—Zee, and nothing else.

Inside the folder were a few pages of printed text. It began with *To my sons...*

As Sebastian read his father's words tears formed. He clasped Roman's hand. The old man had had a change of heart. Elaine, and the strokes, had been the catalyst to opening his eyes. To seeing his family in a new way. He didn't want to someday pit his youngest sons against one another. He regretted doing as much with Sebastian and Philippe. It had been what he'd known. There was no way to take back the years. But he wanted to move forward in a new way. To learn a new way. He intended to ask Elaine to marry him. He would surprise her in a few days.

Sebastian nodded with joy. This really was a change for his father!

"Read the back," Roman said.

Sebastian turned over the page.

I watched you at the family dinner. The way you looked at Mademoiselle Grace. You admire her. You respect her. I've never seen you look at a woman that way.

Sebastian swallowed back a tear as he nodded, "I do admire her. Everything about her is everything to my heart. I love her."

He read the remainder.

I want to earn that same look of respect and admiration from you, my son. Someday.

Another nod. It was all he could do not to blurt, "Yes, someday, I want to look at you in that manner." It would happen. This family could change. And it would begin with this letter.

It made Sebastian's heart swell to read the next lines that detailed how Roman intended to dissolve the competition. And he wanted both his sons to agree to what he'd decided.

Sebastian stood and leaned over to hug his father. It didn't feel unnatural. Because he'd had some practice with Zee. "I love you, *mon père*. We can do this. As a family."

A week after Dahlia left, Azalea sat on the stone patio out back of the house, finishing a braided daisy crown. A pile of uprooted weeds sat to her left. The plants with the little yellow flowers remained untouched. Though she suspected they might also be weeds, they were too pretty to pull up. And she liked how they spread across the stones forming a soft carpet for her bare feet. Later, she'd surf online to find out what they were and if there were uses for them such as a natural elixir or even tea. Since settling into the château, she'd become all about using what the land gave her and DIY-ing the heck out of things. It was fun and gave her a sense of satisfaction.

She set the circlet crown on her head. "Rural princess!" she declared to the symphony of crickets. "Well, you don't have to bow, but I would appreciate a little less chirping come late night."

And thinking about noisy animals… Now, to get some chickens for the little coop that sat beside the barn. Fresh eggs every morning? She was living the life.

Sebastian had texted her this morning. He intended to stop in tomorrow and wanted to know if she needed anything. She'd given him a list of foods that she hadn't a chance to get to the grocery store for, despite the little car that had been stored in the garage for over a decade and which ran like a dream. Milk, eggs and lots of chocolate pastries. She was labeling it a pregnancy craving, but really? She just loved pastries.

She'd added "live chickens" to the list but did not expect that one to actually be fulfilled.

With a satisfied sigh, she tilted her head to take the sunshine into her pores. She could do this. She was doing this. It felt right, like the thing that had been waiting for her to finally turn around and declare, "Oh, yes, that's for me!" Her aspirations to find a job had slipped away. Supporting herself completely wasn't doable at the present moment. In a few years, she'd revisit her goals and desires and if a job felt right then, she'd explore her options.

Yet she knew the country life was not something that Sebastian could get behind. Visits on the weekend might be all he could manage, or even want. The man had an important job that kept him at the office and in the city where he needed to meet with contacts face-to-face. He thrived on the busyness of Paris.

He might feel obligated to treat her as a girlfriend since she was having his child. But he couldn't sustain that forever. Could he? Perhaps she should tell him he should start dating so he could find a wife and win that CEO position? The competition did not stipulate the wife and baby had to be from the same person. And really, Roman Mercier should be proud his son was spreading his DNA around.

She could be okay with that.

Sighing, she shook her head. "You love him. Don't deny it. You got pregnant by the rebound guy and now he's taken over your heart."

Time to start listening to her heart.

If she was to be true to her heart, she needed to make it clear to Sebastian that she did love him. To, well, to fight for him. If they did marry it could be good. It could be real and based on love and caring for one another. It wouldn't have to be simply because of the competition. And if part of it was? Then she was going into the marriage eyes wide-open.

"I'm denying him an easy win if I insist we never marry," she said. "I want him to win. The CEO position will make him happy."

With a sense of renewed purpose, she nodded. Tomorrow she was going to ask Sebastian to marry her. Hopefully, it would be the best choice she had ever made.

CHAPTER TWENTY

SEBASTIAN WAS ARRIVING this morning. And Azalea had a plan. She'd picked wildflowers from the overgrown field behind the barn. Armloads of them. Now she stepped back from the front stoop, looking over her work. The azaleas had shed their blossoms weeks ago. She'd managed to create a bough of wildflowers cascading over the entryway. It looked lush and romantic and smelled like heaven. Here was where she'd ask him to marry her.

"It could work," she whispered with hope.

No woman was going to share her baby daddy's surname but her. Azalea Mercier had a certain ring to it.

"A ring?" A proposal wasn't a proposal without one. "Dash it. I need to find something…"

She wandered barefoot around the side of the château. The grass was soft and freshly mown thanks to the grounds crew that stopped by once every two weeks. She plucked up the daisy crown she'd made yesterday and placed it on her head.

If he said yes. Would he? She couldn't know what his answer would be. Their lives had been altered with this pregnancy. Their needs and desires had been brought to the fore, amplified. Perhaps he wouldn't be willing to commit if she demanded real love from him?

Mostly, she wished he'd just walk back into her life, kiss her silly, make love to her until they were sated, and stake his claim to her. That was how it happened in the movies.

"Life is not a movie," she muttered. Plucking a daisy, she decapitated the white-petaled head. "This rural princess has to work a miracle if she intends to win her prince."

She busied herself with creating a ring from the stem.

When the sound of a large vehicle rolling down the drive turned her head, she dropped the daisy stem and wandered around from the backyard to see a truck backing up to the gravel side lot before the barn.

A livestock trailer? She hadn't ordered any animals. Though the barn was clean and ready to receive any stock she might wish to own. She'd already looked into finding a rescue animal, or two, in the area.

The driver got out of the truck and—

"Dad?" She rushed up to meet Oliver Grace, who sported a big smile and wrapped her in an even bigger hug. "I don't understand?"

"Hey, sweetie." He gave her tummy a pat. "You look beautiful. Wow, it's nice out here, isn't it? Diane and I will have to spend a weekend with you sometime."

"You are always welcome."

He tapped her crown, then gave her a kiss on the nose where once he'd teased that each kiss added another freckle.

"I'm glad you decided to stop in for a visit, but I don't understand why you're here? What's in the truck?"

He held up a finger. "I've brought you a few things that I know are important to you. Hang on." With that, he opened the back of the trailer and pulled down a ramp, walked up it and opened an inner gate. He then guided down a cow. And it wasn't just any cow.

"Stella?" Azalea took the reins from him as he again disappeared inside the truck, where she saw another smaller cow. "Daisy! But how? I thought you sold them, Dad?"

"I did." He shrugged. "But someone bought them back because he knew how much they meant to you. That's the other important thing I brought today." He leaned back and slapped the metal side of the truck. "Hup!"

A door slammed and from around the front of the truck walked another man, wearing sunglasses and an expensive suit perfectly fitted to accentuate his physique. On his feet were wellies. A rather stylish pair with a designer logo splashed around the tops. And he carried something she would have never thought to see a man in a suit carry. A chicken with lustrous brown feathers that gleamed blue in the sunlight.

Azalea handed the reins to her dad as she gaped at the sight of the new arrival. "Sebastian?"

"You were expecting me, yes?"

"Of course, but…. What is this?" She looked to her dad, who smiled widely but offered no explanation. But of course! She'd written *live chickens* on her grocery list. And he'd actually come through? What a guy!

"I talked to your dad days ago," Sebastian explained. "Asked him something important and… he told me *no*. It made me do a lot of thinking."

"I have no clue what you're talking about. You two are in cahoots?"

"That's a good way to put it." Sebastian pushed his sunglasses to the top of his head and winked at her dad. "That conversation with Oliver sent me to my father's doorstep and we had a long and good conversation. My dad has had a change of heart. The strokes have him viewing his life and his family with new eyes. He proposed to Elaine last night."

"Really? That's amazing. That's good, right?"

"It's incredible. She's taught an old dog a new trick. Elaine insists the twins do not grow up like Philippe and I have. Always competing. Dad agreed."

"He did? But that's..."

"That's what led him to dissolve the competition for the CEO position."

"But—Sebastian, you wanted that position. Now what happens?"

"Now Philippe is going step into the role of CEO of the new company Dad wants to form. A women's atelier. It will be completely separate from L'Homme Mercier. As it should be. And I will take the reins of L'Homme Mercier."

"You got the position!" She plunged forward for a hug but stopped abruptly as the chicken in his arms clucked. "It's what you deserve. I'm so glad your dad had a change of heart. And to celebrate you brought me the chicken I asked for."

"Actually, it's more than that."

Sebastian stroked the calm chicken. Its feathers were sheened blue and green and his strokes revealed a bright orange undertone as the soft feathers moved. The fowl was perfectly content on his arm.

It was almost too much to take in. And now

she noticed his wellies had a splotch of chicken doo-doo on them. The man was out of his element. And yet, he fit in like a shiny new garden implement just waiting to be dirtied a little.

She looked to her dad, who still wasn't offering any explanation, not even a helpful gesture. The two of them had been talking? This was crazy!

"Of course, Stella and Daisy will love the field," she offered, unsure what else to say. "And there's the old chicken coop beside the barn, but..."

"But there's something more." Sebastian approached her. He held the chicken as any experienced farmer would cradle a cherished farm animal. Now he bent a knee and kneeled before her. "It's a proposal."

A pro—? But she had planned to— She'd dropped her makeshift ring upon hearing the trailer drive up. Azalea's breath gasped out as she slapped her chest. Her dad nodded, smiling widely. She wasn't sure how he was involved, but did it matter?

Sebastian, on one knee, held up the chicken in offering between them and said, "Azalea Grace, you've changed my world and my heart. I don't want to spend a day without you. I want you in my life because I love you. Because we have fun together. Because I want to dance with you until our knees creak and we can no longer move. I asked your dad permission to ask you to marry me and he said no."

With a gape, she looked to her dad.

Oliver shrugged. "He was going to refuse the CEO position and concede to his brother. I knew he loved you, and you loved him, but I also knew he wouldn't be happy. I couldn't let him ask you if it meant he wouldn't be happy."

"That's why I talked to my dad," Sebastian said. "I had to make him understand that you had won my heart, but I also knew your dad was right, that I wouldn't be completely happy if L'Homme Mercier went to Philippe. I told him all that, and then he showed me the letter he'd written stating all the plans he had for dividing the company. As well, we…shared a hug."

His smile now seemed to surprise him. Azalea understood exactly what that hug must have meant to him.

"Anyway…" He held up the chicken before her, a grand gesture if there was one. "Would you accept this chicken from me and say yes to becoming my wife?"

Azalea clasped her hands over her heart. The proposal was absolutely perfect. And everything she wanted from him. And…she glanced to the flowers hanging over the entry. Like nothing she could have imagined or planned. And that her father was here to witness made it even more special.

Still holding out the chicken, Sebastian waited for her reply.

The proposal was genuine and real. It was the most enduring gesture he could have made. And she'd already decided how her best future could look.

The chicken cooed. Sebastian tilted it to look at its little face and cooed back at it. "She'll say yes. She has to." He held the bird higher for her to inspect. "Is the chicken not enough?"

"The chicken is perfect." She took it from him and it settled in the crook of her arm and on her belly as if the bird knew there was a baby inside and it needed to nest and protect it. "You know the way to my heart, Sebastian."

He embraced her gently, including the chicken. "Do you love me?" he asked.

"I do."

"And I love you. I wouldn't have worn rubber boots and traveled for an hour with a chicken in my arms for anyone but you. Will you be my wife? Will you live with me here in the château, but also in Paris? I've already figured I can work four days a week. We can make our schedules work. Maybe you'll live in Paris a few days and then back on the weekends to the country, where you can wear your rural princess crown as I see you've already begun?"

She blushed and tilted down her head. Yes, she had created the crown and wore it with pride.

"I'll do anything to be with you, Zee. Can you be okay with me working but being home every night in your arms? Will you share our boy's life with me?"

Our boy.

Those words landed in her heart and swelled to her extremities with the most wondrous joy.

"I will." She held up her hand, pinkie crooked. He entwined his pinkie with hers. "I love you, Sebastian. And I want to make a family with you."

Their kiss was sweet, indulgent, welcoming, and laced with a thrill of desire. It was the perfect representation of the future that waited them.

The chicken crowed and leaped to the ground. Stella nudged Azalea's arm. And her dad said casually, "Well, that's a bit of all right."

Azalea's heart fluttered. "I'm going to marry you."

"That's the plan."

"Can we get married here? Next summer after the baby is born?"

Sebastian took her in his arms and spun her. "Anything for you, Zee. Oh." He patted his suit pocket. "Almost forgot." Reaching inside his coat, he pulled out and revealed a big, sparkling diamond ring. "You didn't think I'd expect you to wear a chicken on your finger, did you?"

EPILOGUE

The following summer

THE WEDDING WAS a simple affair catered by a posh restaurant for the few dozen people who had come to celebrate Sebastian and Azalea. Now four months old, Zachary Mercier had won the day by attracting the attention of everyone by simply existing. Cute baby wearing a polka-dotted onesie sleeping on a blanket under the willow tree? Haul out the cameras!

The twins were not to be outdone. They attracted as many photo opportunities and were currently tearing apart pansies and nibbling on the petals. Roman and Elaine, who had married over Christmas, were contemplating house hunting in the south of France now that Roman was completely retired. Oliver and Diane were headed almost the same direction, to Spain, for a few weeks before then trekking to Hawaii.

After most of the guests had left, and only

their closest family lingered in the château—some staying the night in the guest rooms—Sebastian and Azalea danced slowly on the patio to the music of their hearts. Zachary slept quietly in his nearby cradle, rocked gently by the breeze. Sunday, the chicken—because Sebastian had proposed on a Sunday—was perched on the bow of the cradle, her favorite place to rest when the baby slept.

The moon was full and bright. The summer air just right. Sebastian had shed his suit coat and unbuttoned his collar. Azalea's pink spaghetti-strap dress dusted the grass because she'd not worn shoes all day. Her hair spilled in thick curls—thanks to Dahlia's styling—and was circled with a frothy pink crown of her namesake flower.

"You are the most beautiful woman in the world," Sebastian said as they swayed under the moonlight. "You have my heart. And so does Zachary."

"We're doing rather well at this family thing," she said as she rested her head against his shoulder.

Since taking over as CEO, Sebastian had been able to reduce his in-office hours to three days a week, then home to the country for two days day of online work, with the weekend free. Azalea and Zac commuted to Paris for two or three days midweek. She enjoyed the change of pace, which allowed her to stroll Zac around the parks and discover all the endless tourist attractions and hidden wonders of the city.

On the days she was in Paris, the neighbor girl, a sixteen-year-old with dreams of becoming a veterinarian, looked after their livestock and chickens. It was a perfect situation.

"I sometimes wonder," he said softly. "If you hadn't been such a strong and fearless woman, I might have never experienced you charging into the limo. I'm so glad you kicked the photographer and ran to me."

"I'm glad you were there to catch me."

"Always and forever, Zee."

* * * * *

If you enjoyed this story, check out these other great reads from Michele Renae: